MW00904723

dangerous crossings!

true stories from the edge

Look for more exciting titles in the award-winning series, **True Stories from the Edge:**

Thieves! by Andreas Schroeder

Of all the crimes people commit, stealing is the most common. These stories of incredible heists explore the realm of serious criminals, from the notorious to the strangely heart-warming.

Scams! by Andreas Schroeder

Scam artists have been tricking people for a very long time. These dramatic stories include some of the most outrageous and inventive swindlers of all time.

Rescues! by Tanya Lloyd Kyi

Join desperate rescuers as they race through landslides, dangle over cliffs, and dive to the ocean floor. Witness real-life heroes as they brave flames, fly into uncharted territory, and defy deadly gunmen.

Fires! by Tanya Lloyd Kyi

Step into the blinding flames, the choking smoke, and the waves of heat that brought humans face to face with one of the world's mightiest natural forces.

Tunnels! by Diane Swanson

People have been tunneling since the Stone Age. These gripping stories of human drama beneath the ground are fast-paced and tension-filled.

Escapes! by Laura Scandiffio

History is full of daring escapes. The exhilarating stories in this collection take readers around the world and across the ages.

true stories from the edge

Antonia Banyard

dangerous crossings!

Ten daring treks
across land, sea,
and air

toronto + new york + vancouver

Text © 2007 Antonia Banyard

Annick Press Ltd.
All rights reserved. No part of this work covered by the copyrights hereon may be reproduced or used in any form or by any means—graphic, electronic, or mechanical—without prior written permission of the publisher.

We acknowledge the support of the Canada Council for the Arts, the Ontario Arts Council, the Government of Canada through the Book Publishing Industry Development Program (BPIDP), and the Ontario Book Publishing Tax Credit (OBPTC) for our publishing activities.

Edited by Pam Robertson
Copy edited by Elizabeth McLean
Cover and interior design by Irvin Cheung / iCheung Design, inc.
Cover illustration: Scott Cameron
Maps: Antonia Banyard, basic outlines by Map Resources. For illustration purposes only.

Cataloguing in Publication
Banyard, Antonia
        Dangerous crossings! / by Antonia Banyard.

(True stories from the edge)
Includes bibliographical references and index.
ISBN 978-1-55451-086-3 (bound)
ISBN 978-1-55451-085-6 (pbk.)

        1. Adventure and adventurers—Juvenile literature. 2. Voyages and travel—Juvenile literature. I. Title. II. Series.
G175.B36 2007   j910'.922   C2007-902946-9

Printed and bound in Canada

Published in the U.S.A. by	Distributed in Canada by	Distributed in the U.S.A. by
Annick Press (U.S.) Ltd.	Firefly Books Ltd.	Firefly Books (U.S.) Inc.
	66 Leek Crescent	P.O. Box 1338
	Richmond Hill, ON	Ellicott Station
	L4B 1H1	Buffalo, NY 14205

Visit our website at **www.annickpress.com**

Contents

Introduction:

To the Ends of the Earth

"The world is a book and those who do not travel read only a page."
— St. Augustine, 354–430 CE

IF YOUR PARENTS SUDDENLY ANNOUNCED a family trip, you'd be excited, right? Or would you worry about missing your friends and eating strange food? Some people can't wait to board a plane, while for others, crossing town is enough excitement. For those of us in the first group, what is travel's appeal, anyway?

There are as many reasons to seek adventure as there are travelers—a few of which you'll read about in the following stories. One reason is simply to return home. One of the words for a long journey, *odyssey*, comes from an epic poem of the same name.

The Odyssey was written 2600 years ago by the Greek poet Homer. It describes the 10-year sea journey made by a Greek king, Odysseus, from Troy in northwest Turkey to his home in Ithaca, a tiny island in the Ionian Sea. Along the way, Odysseus encounters beings beyond his wildest imaginings, such as one-eyed giants (the Cyclops). His adventures include a visit to the Underworld, though luckily he makes it back to the land of the living. He's delayed by vengeful gods and goddesses who imprison him or wreck his boat, and helped by beautiful maidens. By the time he gets home, not even his wife, Penelope, recognizes him.

The appeal of home, or the relief of sleeping in our own beds again, can be just as delicious as adventures on the road. But some people love staying away from home or travel so much that they don't even have a home. The list of those who have traveled for the sake of travel, and become famous for it, is long.

One such man was English adventurer and explorer Sir Richard Burton, who spent most of the mid- to late 1800s in foreign countries. He knew enough languages to boggle the mind—29, by one count. Not only did he adopt local languages, but the dress and mannerisms as well. He'd often disguise himself to visit places he otherwise wouldn't be able to enter. Burton even persuaded the Royal Geographical Society to fund his journey to the Islamic holy city of Mecca (or Makkah)—where non-Muslims are not allowed. While he wasn't the first non-Muslim to go (in disguise, of course), he became the most famous.

Burton lived in an era when Europeans were crazy about mapping the world. But once the map had been mostly filled in, adventurers set out to solve new geographical mysteries, such as rediscovering the lost city of Machu Picchu in Peru, or digging through Egyptian pyramids, or climbing Mount Everest. Within a hundred years, the world wasn't enough, and Americans Neil Armstrong and Buzz Aldrin headed for the moon.

Apart from curiosity or the thirst for knowledge, people leave home out of necessity, in wartime, for instance. During the Second World War, Gerda Weissmann, a young Jewish-Polish girl, was taken from her home and sent to a series of Nazi labor camps. Toward the end of the war, Weissmann and the other inmates were marched across Germany to avoid the Allied troops advancing eastward. After more than 560 kilometers (350 miles), they were liberated in Czechoslovakia by the US Army. The 21-year-old Gerda weighed a mere 31 kilograms (68 pounds). She discovered that her whole family had been killed except for one uncle. Since then, Gerda Weissmann Klein, who now lives in the US, has written memoirs about her experiences.

In another era and on the other side of the world, Var Hong Ashe experienced a journey with many parallels to Weissmann Klein's. In April 1975, Var Hong was a teacher in the capital of Cambodia, Phnom Penh. The country had just been through a five-year civil war, won by the Khmer Rouge, a Communist guerilla organization. At first Var Hong welcomed the victors, hoping for an end to the war. But within hours after entering Phnom Penh, the Khmer Rouge ordered everyone to leave. Var Hong, her mother, three sisters, two brothers, and her two daughters left their home. For four years, the Khmer Rouge marched them from village to village where the prisoners dug irrigation canals or planted rice.

Var Hong later discovered that the Khmer Rouge's goal was to eliminate all rich or educated people—who mostly lived in cities. She survived by pretending to be ignorant, and through sheer willpower. She ended up in a small jungle village near the Cambodia-Thailand border. With a sister and her two daughters, she walked to a refugee camp in Thailand—free at last.

THE DESIRE FOR KNOWLEDGE is another reason for setting off into the unknown. Some will even break the law to find out what they want to know. The insatiable curiosity of a Chinese Buddhist monk resulted in a 16-year trek across inhospitable deserts, towering mountain ranges, and raging rivers. In 629, Hsuan Tsang (or Xuanzang) decided that the Chinese understanding of Buddhism was incomplete because they did not possess all of the holy writings, and the translations were sometimes conflicting. He wanted to study in India, the birthplace of Buddhism.

At that time, an imperial ban forbade anyone from traveling past the Jade Gate on the eastern edge of Chinese territory. So Hsuan Tsang had to break the law just to start his journey, sneaking out in the middle of the night. This law-breaking monk nearly lost his life, as imperial police followed him closely. He was able to shake them by entering the Gobi Desert, which everyone declared was impossible to cross. As he later related, he survived through faith and by following his horse—who, by instinct, led him to an oasis.

Hsuan Tsang succeeded in his goal—encountering bandits, murderous Hindu priests, and royalty along the way. Whether it was on foot, horseback, camel-back, or elephant-back, he crossed about 8000 kilometers (5000 miles) before returning home. For the rest of his days, he wrote about his journeys and what he had learned.

People still travel to learn or discover. An Englishman, John Hare, got hooked on camels in 1999 during an expedition to the Gashun Gobi—part of the same desert that Hsuan Tsang crossed. Hare was looking for the near-extinct Bactrian camel, believed to be the genetic great-grandpappy of all camels on earth. Not only is the desert remote, it's not a particularly comfortable or entertaining place. For weeks, Hare, seven Chinese researchers, and 20 pack camels gazed at sand dune after dusty sand dune. But eventually they did spot a pair of shaggy two-humped Bactrian camels. By the end of Hare's trip, they'd seen about one-fifth of the world's Bactrian camel population (about 900). The dedicated Hare, with his Chinese counterparts, helped to establish one of the world's largest nature sanctuaries, the 150,000-square-kilometer (58,000-square-mile) Arjin Shan Lop Nur Wild Camel Reserve.

JOHN HARE IS ONE OF A NEW BREED OF TRAVELERS, those who travel for a cause. Wade Davis, a Canadian ethnobotanist (someone who studies the traditional knowledge and customs of a people), has used his travels to Borneo to campaign for the Penan people, who are not only losing their traditional land, but their language and culture along with it.

An extraordinary journey gets attention, so some trekkers combine the novelty of their voyage with worthy causes. In 2004, for example, Polly Letofsky returned to her hometown of Vail, Colorado after a five-year walk around the world to raise money for breast cancer research.

Then there are the wacky travelers, the record-breakers and first-timers. In 1989, a couple from Calcutta, Mohammed and Neena Salahuddin Choudhury, drove around the world by car in a record-breaking 69 days and 19 hours. When a British team made the journey in less time, the Choudhurys climbed into their jeep and cut their first record almost in half—to 39 days and 20 hours.

There's even a medical term for people with a compulsive urge to travel. They're called dromomaniacs, and Heinz Stucke may be one of them. In 1962 the German tool- and die-maker decided he needed to see something new, so he got on his bike and cycled out of town. More than 40 years later, he's still pedaling. So far the 66-year-old has covered more than 668,000 kilometers (415,000 miles)—that's the same as circling the globe nearly 17 times.

Journeys, treks, and expeditions fascinate us so much, they've spawned whole genres and subcultures: travel stories, documentaries, clubs, and networks. For every great trip (and those terrible ones), there's a great story. The people in these 10 stories try to get home, find something new, or go where no one has gone before. Luckily, armchair travelers like us can join in their adventures from the comfort of the living room couch.

A Long Walk Home

Western Australia, August–October 1931

BY HER SECOND NIGHT at the Moore River Native Settlement, Molly Craig had had enough. She'd leave the next morning and take her sisters with her.

They'd thought that the Settlement was a school and that they'd only have to stay there awhile before going back home. But as Molly lay in bed and listened to the padlock rattle, she knew this was no school. That rattle was the sound of the staff locking her and the other girls inside. The girls' dormitory had bars on the windows, bolts and chains on the doors, and cold hard beds. Instead of a toilet, there was a bucket in one corner for them to use during the night. When she'd first seen the building, Molly thought it looked like a jail. It felt like one too.

She and her sisters, Gracie Cross and Daisy Burungu, huddled together on one bed, sharing their blankets for warmth. The girls' mothers were sisters, but following Aboriginal tradition, the girls considered themselves sisters too, not cousins. They were in this together.

After falling asleep, Molly dreamed of home.

A COUPLE OF WEEKS EARLIER, the three girls had been taken from their families by the district Protector of Aborigines in northern Western Australia. Molly, Gracie, and Daisy were *muda-muda* children, meaning that their fathers were white and their mothers Australian Aboriginals. Most *muda-mudas* grew up in the bush with their mothers, although some fathers, like Molly's and Gracie's, kept in touch. The girls grew up as Aboriginals.

The white government shared the racist views that were common at the time: officials felt these children were not safe in the Aboriginal communities and that only white people could care for them properly. Also, many believed that whites were naturally smarter than Aboriginals, although the part-white children might be "smart" enough to work as maids, cooks, or stockmen for ranchers. But they could only learn Western ways if they were taken away from their Aboriginal families.

For that reason, *muda-muda* children were considered wards of the state—literally orphans, whether they had parents or not—and the Chief Protector was their legal guardian. His job was to find the children and send them to settlements like Moore River. One Protector claimed that Aboriginal people forgot about their offspring anyway! Even the white fathers couldn't stop their children from being taken away—they'd be thrown into jail for trying.

In Western Australia, the Chief Protector was Mr. A. O. Neville. The Aboriginals certainly didn't think Mr. Neville was protecting them. They also never forgot their children, of course, although at first some parents didn't realize that they'd never see them again. The children didn't know that almost everything they did would be monitored and controlled by the white authorities: where they worked, who they married, where they traveled. Most never saw their families again.

When the children at the Settlement were told their mothers had forgotten them, Molly knew this wasn't true. She and her mother were both longing to be reunited.

The morning after Molly decided to escape the Moore River Settlement, the girls were shaken awake before the sun was even up. Molly, Gracie, and Daisy followed the others to the dining hall and ate a breakfast of bug-infested porridge, bread, and bitter tea.

When the school bell rang, the other girls rushed off to classes. "Don't be late on your first day!" one bossy girl said to Molly.

"We'll come after we empty the toilet bucket," she answered. But once the others were gone, she told her sisters to grab their things. "We're not going to school today, we're going home to Jigalong." The other two stared at her in amazement. "Hurry up," Molly said. They had to get as far away as possible before anyone discovered they'd gone.

"But how?" Daisy asked. "It's a long way." It had taken them many days by boat, then hours by car to travel from Jigalong in the state's far north to Moore River in the south. How could they find their way back, much less walk all that distance?

"I know it's far," Molly said in her most confident, 14-year-old voice. "But it'll be easy. We'll find the rabbit-proof fence, then follow that home."

Three barbed-wire fences made up the "rabbit-proof fence." The first one built, called No. 1, ran from the top of Western Australia to the bottom, drawing a line 1833 kilometers (1139 miles) down the state. The other two fences were built as additions. When the white people first came to Australia, they brought their animals with them: rabbits, cows, sheep, and foxes. The hot, dry country suited the rabbits well and they multiplied. And multiplied. With no natural predators, they soon overran the island continent, digging burrows and nibbling every green leaf they could.

The three fences, completed in 1907, were meant to prevent rabbits from spreading farther west. At periodic outposts along the fence, crews were stationed to fix broken wire, fallen stakes, or remove the many animals that perished on the barbed wire.

The Jigalong government depot lay west of the No. 1 fence. The way home was simple, Molly thought. They just had to find the fence and soon they'd be home.

Eight-year-old Daisy and eleven-year-old Gracie were used to following their older sister, so they bundled their few possessions into cloth bags. Grabbing the toilet bucket, they hurried across the grounds. After dumping it, they ran toward the river that flowed behind the dormitory.

Their first challenge was to cross the fast current. After a few unsuccessful attempts, Molly found a tall gum tree by the bank. It leaned far over the water. They carefully climbed up its trunk, then, hanging onto one of its branches, swung down to the other bank. For the next two hours, they scrambled along the slippery, muddy banks.

"Okay now," Molly said. "We'll go north now, the rest of the way." They had no time to lose.

Only the day before, one of the girls had told her what happened to children who tried to escape. Those who'd made the attempt had walked to the nearby train tracks. They'd waited in the spot where the trains slowed down, then jumped onto a passing car. But the Aboriginal tracker always caught them. After whipping them, he'd take them back to Moore River where they were locked up for days, with only bread and water. Their heads were shaved, they were paraded in front of the others, and lashed with a leather strap. No one had run away without being caught.

As Molly and her sisters headed into the bush, they set out east, in the direction of the No. 1 fence. Day after day, they walked.

WHEN MOLLY SAW THE FENCE, she let out an excited yelp. "We're nearly home!" she called out to her two sisters, who lagged behind. She touched the wire and felt truly hopeful for the first time in days. It would be so good to see her family, to hear her mother's voice.

The three had been walking for a month already, through fields and open bush, from dawn till dusk every day. Molly had known that the easy route—catching the train—would never work. They'd just be caught like the other kids. Walking through the bush was harder, but safer—so far. When they got really tired, Molly gave her sisters piggybacks, one at a time. Their legs, scratched from scrambling through thickets of acacia thorn bushes, were now covered in painful sores. Though tired and hungry, they were happy to see the fence at last.

They were now skirting the edge of the Western Desert, a vast expanse of smaller connecting deserts. To the European settlers, the desert was hot, bare, and inhospitable. But where the white settlers saw a barren wasteland, for children whose ancestors had lived there for thousands of years, it was a welcoming place. In their eyes, it was filled with enough water and food to fill every need. They could find water holes, yams, fruits, and seeds, or kill small animals such as frogs or goana lizards.

Even so far from home, in a completely new territory, Molly and her sisters could survive. They knew how to tell when water was safe to drink and how to test which plants were edible. They could hunt for birds or lizards, and gut and skin a rabbit and have it roasting on a stick in no time. Not only that, Molly could navigate by the sun, even after it had disappeared behind rain clouds.

They'd learned these skills when their families periodically moved camp from the government depot out to the bush. Catching and cooking "bush tucker," or wild food, was fine enough, but it was also a lot of work. And sometimes, there was nothing to catch.

They'd survived so far because of their bush smarts, but also due to the kindness of farmers along the way. When the girls came to a farmhouse, Molly, knowing the authorities would be looking for three girls, would send Daisy and Gracie to knock on the door and ask for food. If they were welcomed, Molly would climb out from her hiding place and join them. They were never turned away, and most often the farmers would send them off with a packet of food.

Even so, Molly was worried. They had no adults to guide them or care for them. There were always dangers out in the bush. Every morning they woke up wondering if they'd find any food, or be alive by the end of the day.

Luckily, they were traveling during the rainy season, when plants flourished and animals grew fat. Grass grew thick and tall around the fence. The rains in the region had been good, adorning their desert surroundings with flashes of color. Flowers like red or yellow pompoms covered the gum trees. Different species of banksia had bright bottlebrush flowers sticking straight up from the branches. Red and green flowers waved among the leaves of kangaroo paw plants.

Once they found the No. 1 fence, the girls were confident that their journey was almost over. What the girls didn't realize was that they were still far from home. Their journey, straight north along the fence, would mean another 800 kilometers (500 miles).

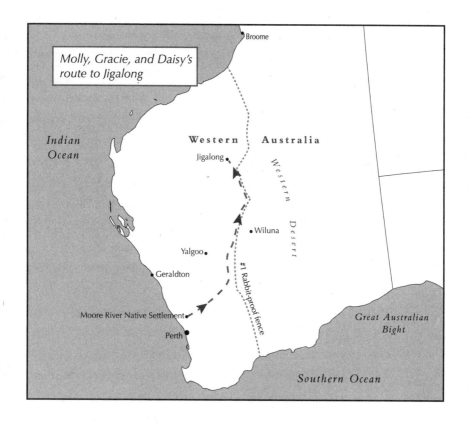

Molly, Gracie, and Daisy's route to Jigalong

Broome

Indian Ocean

Western   Australia

Jigalong

W e s t e r n

D e s e r t

Wiluna

Yalgoo

Geraldton

#1 Rabbit-proof fence

Moore River Native Settlement

Perth

Great Australian Bight

Southern Ocean

"HEY, YOU GIRLS. WAIT!"

It was a man's voice. In an instant, the girls were hidden under an acacia bush. They could see an Aboriginal man biking toward them, shouting and waving something.

"I've got food," he called out.

Peeking through the bushes, the girls gazed longingly at the bread and tinned meat in his hand. "Don't be frightened," he said.

Their stomachs rumbled. Finally hunger overcame fear and they crawled out into the open.

As they ate, the man introduced himself. He worked at Pindathuna, the nearby cattle station. Still a little wary, they told him they were headed for Wiluna, a nearby train station. Feeling better for the food in their stomachs, the girls said goodbye and continued on.

The stockman, Don Willocks, had heard in the news about the three girls who'd escaped the Moore River Settlement. He was glad to see they were doing well after all, but after saying goodbye, he began to worry for their safety. He reported the encounter to his boss, telling him the direction the girls were headed. His boss then telephoned the police station in Yalgoo, just west of the ranch. In turn, the police constable at Yalgoo called the inspector in the west coast town of Geraldton.

Soon a tracker was brought to Yalgoo. Trackers knew the bush intimately and could find a trail by reading the faintest tracks in the dust, or almost imperceptible markings on plants or rocks the girls had passed by. For two days, the tracker, police constable, and Don searched along the fence, heading north from the spot where Don had met the girls. They found no trail—recent rain had washed away the tracks. On the third day, they gave up.

The men didn't know that the girls had backtracked in search of bush tucker. Molly, Daisy, and Gracie never knew how close they'd come to capture. They were also unaware that many of the kind farmers, worried for their safety just as Don had been, had been reporting them to the local police.

Other search parties were sent out, but the rains meant that the muddy roads were impossible to negotiate by car. Also working in the girls' favor was the sheer vastness of the land and the fact that it was so sparsely populated.

The authorities were determined to capture the girls and had been given permission from the Chief Protector of Aborigines to spend whatever it took to find them. If three little "half-caste" girls could foil the efforts of grown men (mostly white), it would not only be embarrassing, it might give other homesick children ideas.

Miraculously, Molly, Daisy, and Gracie had slipped past every search party that had been sent out—so far.

After they met Don, though, they somehow sensed that they were no longer safe, so they didn't dare approach any more farmhouses.

Picking up their pace, they continued north, sleeping only a few hours a night. If they caught an animal, they didn't even stop to cook it, but ate the raw meat as they trudged along.

ALTHOUGH MOLLY CONTINUED ON at a relentless speed, Gracie was getting tired. Her legs ached and she didn't like being hungry. Maybe living in the Settlement wouldn't be so bad after all, she thought. At least she would have a bed to sleep in and three meals a day, even if she had to pick out the odd bug.

She'd had enough.

Finally, they came to a spot near a small, isolated train station. There had to be people working there, Gracie declared. "I'm going to see them." Even though she knew she could be caught, she marched toward the station. When she returned, her face was lit with excitement. A *muda-muda* woman there said that her mother was now living nearby, in Wiluna. When the train came, Gracie would take it to join her mother.

Her sisters pleaded with her to stay with them. The police might see her at the train station. And Molly didn't want them to be separated.

But Gracie's feet were sore. The train sounded much more appealing than following endless fence posts.

"I don't want to die," she said, turning her back on her sisters.

Molly knew it was dangerous to linger. Besides, Gracie's mind was made up. Hurt and sad, she and Daisy had to say goodbye.

By noon that day, the sun was blisteringly hot. Molly was exhausted, as much from her argument with Gracie as from the heat or the walking. She and Daisy found a place by the river and she lay down and slept.

Meanwhile, Daisy climbed a tree and found some young birds to eat. Climbing down, she scratched her knee and yelped in pain.

A young station worker nearby heard her. Right away, he knew she was one of the escaped children he'd heard about, so he called her over. In a harsh, demanding way, he told her to bring her sisters to him.

Daisy, frightened and still mad about her cut knee, swore at him, then started throwing stones. He was big and not at all friendly.

The young man, ducking the flying stones, climbed back onto his horse. "All right, you wait," he cried as he galloped off. "I'm going to report you to the police!"

The shouting woke up Molly, who came running. When Daisy told her what had happened, she knew they had to get away, quickly.

By this time, the days were getting longer. As long as there was enough light to see by, they pushed on. Now in their home region, the Pilbara, they recognized places they'd been with their families.

They could name the birds and butterflies, and the wide-open stretches dotted with tufts of spiny-leaved grasses looked familiar. White-barked ghost gum trees made a stark contrast to the deep blue sky and red-dirt termite mounds. They knew exactly where they were going. Their excitement grew with each day.

One evening, they could tell they were just south of cattle station 594, near the camp of some relatives. Although they tried, they couldn't make it all the way and had to lie down for a while before continuing on. Guided by the bright moon, they walked until exhaustion overcame them.

The next day they woke up hungry but determined. At the sight of the station, they wanted to run, but were too weak and had to drag themselves along the last stretch.

At the campsite, they found one of Molly's aunts. She wept as they told her their story. "You silly girls," she cried. "You could have died in the bush and no one would have known!"

When they were given dinner, Molly and Daisy could hardly eat any—their stomachs had shrunk. But they were happy to reach safety and relieved to be so close to home. That night, lying in a comfortable bed for the first time in almost nine weeks, they slept soundly.

It was only three or four days' walk from Jigalong, but they were with family now and didn't have to walk alone. Their cousin and his boss were traveling by camel in the same direction, so the girls joined them. What they didn't know was that a messenger had been sent ahead to tell their family the happy news.

Nervous excitement made them jittery as they walked the last stretch to their mothers' camp. Across the distance, they could hear their families wailing. This was the traditional way to greet long-lost visitors and told them a crowd was waiting, ready to welcome them. After a nearly impossible journey, the girls had made it home at last. It felt almost too good to be true.

DAISY AND MOLLY WALKED an incredible 2400 kilometers (1500 miles) in just over two months. They didn't rest for long, though.

The next morning, their family broke camp and disappeared into the bush to hide from any authorities still searching for the girls.

After the three sisters had parted, Gracie caught the train to Wiluna, only to discover her mother wasn't there. She waited, hoping her mother would return. Unfortunately, a police informer spotted her before she heard anything more about her mother's whereabouts. Before long, she was recaptured and sent back to the Moore River Native Settlement.

The authorities kept a rough record of Molly and Daisy for months afterward, but were unwilling to spend more money on their capture. The three girls had already cost the department a lot. The Chief Protector, Mr. Neville, also feared that Molly and Daisy were unteachable, and had "gone native." This only confirmed in his eyes that children of mixed descent needed to be taken away from their families when they were young.

MANY OF THE *MUDA-MUDA* CHILDREN sent to settlements such as Moore River led difficult lives. They are often called the "Stolen Generation," because they were stolen from their families, and their culture and sense of belonging was stolen from them. Despite their triumph, the story of the three sisters isn't a completely happy one.

Gracie, of course, never saw her family again. But Daisy was lucky. Not long after reuniting with her family, she moved south of Jigalong. After training as a housemaid, she worked at several cattle stations before marrying. She had four girls and eventually retired to Jigalong to live with her children.

As for Molly, her trouble was not over. For a few years, she worked as a maid and cook on a cattle station. She married an Aboriginal man named Toby Kelly and had two girls, Doris and

Annabelle. But then she got appendicitis and was sent to the hospital in Perth, where the authorities found her again. Even though she was a grown woman, she was quickly transported back to the Moore River Settlement, this time with her two children.

After hearing that some of her family had died, Molly escaped from the Settlement a second time. Annabelle was a toddler and Doris was five years old. Molly knew that she could carry Annabelle, but the journey would be too much for Doris. She made the difficult decision to leave her oldest daughter behind, then followed the same route to Jigalong that she'd taken nine years earlier, arriving home safely again.

Three years later, Annabelle was taken away and put into a children's home. Molly lost all contact with her and never saw her again, but fortunately was reunited with Doris late in life.

Doris grew up at the Moore River Settlement, then went on to train first as a nurse and later as a journalist and filmmaker. As an adult, she found her mother and Aunt Daisy, though Gracie had died before Doris could meet her. Doris pieced together the story of her mother and two aunts and recorded it in the book *Follow the Rabbit-Proof Fence*, which was made into a movie.

More importantly, Molly and Daisy's story was told among *muda-muda* children across Western Australia who were imprisoned in settlements. Their story gave other children hope, telling them that their own families hadn't forgotten them, after all.

Rafting across the Pacific

Peru to Polynesia, May–July 1947

"AH, THIS IS THE LIFE," thought Thor Heyerdahl and lay back down on the deck. The sun warmed him from above and waves lapped gently against the raft. His five fellow rafters were passing the time much like he was—loafing. Maybe later he'd try catching a fat gold-finned tunny, or read a book, or maybe he'd just lie here, gazing at the clouds.

Then the wind picked up. A storm was blowing in.

"MAN OVERBOARD!"

All thoughts of the fast-approaching storm vanished at the sound of those words. Heyerdahl could see, just off the bow, his crewmate Herman Watzinger bobbing in the water, and a strange greenish blob swirling in the depths near him. Was it a shark? An unknown creature from the deep? Watzinger's head disappeared behind a rising wave. There was no time to lose.

Heyerdahl rushed across the deck to the dinghy. But even with three men paddling the dinghy, they might not make it back to the raft. Meanwhile, Torstein Raaby grabbed a rope and tossed it to Watzinger, but it only tangled into a knot.

Although Watzinger was a strong swimmer, already the current was quickly carrying the raft away from him. Even swimming his fastest, he'd never catch up. He lunged at the steering oar that stuck out behind. And missed. On board, the rest of the crew scrambled to save their mate. Despite the odds against paddling the dinghy, Heyerdahl and Bengt Danielsson prepared to launch it.

Knut Haugland and Erik Hesselberg threw out the lifebelt, but the strong wind just blew it back on deck. They tried again, to no avail. The wind that foiled their rescue attempts was also filling the sail, taking the raft farther and farther from Watzinger, who bravely swam harder.

Just then, Heyerdahl saw a figure plunge into the water. Haugland held the lifebelt in one hand and pulled himself through the sea with the other. For a few tense moments, they could see first one head rise up on a swell, and then the other. Finally, the two men were together.

When Haugland waved, those on deck pulled on the lifebelt's rope. The two men in the water inched closer, but the dark green shape followed.

As they helped Watzinger and Haugland back on board, the dark shape silently sank into the ocean's depths. They were surprised that Watzinger was sad to see it go—until he told them that the mysterious beast was in fact Raaby's sleeping bag. He'd fallen overboard in the first place trying to save it.

"Glad I wasn't in it," Raaby said, attempting to chuckle. But instead of laughing, the six men looked at each other somberly. That had been a close call. One slip, a few wasted minutes, and Watzinger would have drowned.

They didn't have long to contemplate the danger, however. Black clouds gathered and the wind was building. The storm would soon be on them. Each man knew the drill and went to his post. As night fell, angry waves crashed over the raft's logs.

HEYERDAHL LOOKED AROUND HIM. Who was he kidding? He and the five others weren't simply out for an afternoon's float on a fishing raft. They were in the middle of the Pacific Ocean with nothing around but vast stretches of water and countless sharks. Their raft was the *Kon-Tiki*, built of nine giant balsawood logs and bound with hemp rope. Not much larger than the average living room, its deck was barely higher than the tossing ocean waves. It didn't have a single nail or steel cable to hold it together.

Far from being "the life," Heyerdahl thought. And he was the one who'd got them in this mess. Was he crazy?

Certainly enough people thought so. Before they had launched the *Kon-Tiki* from the port of Callao, Peru, several experienced sailors and navy men had given them tearful good-byes, knowing there was no real hope the six Scandinavians would reach their destination—the Polynesian Islands in the South Pacific—alive. Anyone who'd seen the raft had told them it would sink, that if they ever got out into the ocean, they'd float aimlessly. If they didn't drown or get eaten by sharks, they'd die of exposure.

That was almost six weeks ago. When they'd launched, no one knew how to steer the *Kon-Tiki*, but not because it was a new invention that hadn't been figured out yet. Quite the opposite. According to Heyerdahl's estimation, hundreds of similar rafts had traveled the same journey. The problem was, those knowledgeable rafters had all died 5000 years ago.

So why were the six crewmates trying to mimic these ancient ways? They were following a hunch. For Western anthropologists, it was a great mystery how the thousands of Polynesian islands, scattered across the ocean between South America and Australia, had first been populated. The islands were far from any large land mass, so how had people ever reached them? The accepted theory was that people from Asian civilizations, such as Borneo or Papua New Guinea to the east, had somehow made it across the ocean. But Heyerdahl wasn't convinced.

As a young man, he'd left Norway to live for a year on one of the islands and listened to elders telling their traditional stories. He'd also observed how the clouds always came from the east, and how the waves crashed against the island shores on the east side. According to the Polynesians themselves, their ancestors had come to the islands with the sun, from the east.

Most anthropologists dismissed these traditional stories as myths. But Heyerdahl believed they were grounded in prehistorical truth. He thought Polynesia had first been settled by the indigenous people of Peru, far to the east. Led by their hero Tiki, they had sailed off into the sunset on balsawood rafts just like the one carrying Heyerdahl and his raft mates.

Heyerdahl was so convinced of this that he was willing to risk his life to prove it. He didn't want to learn about ancient people through books and museums, but by experiencing life as they must have experienced it.

Well, he was experiencing it now. The men stood at their posts and hung on tightly. Gale-force winds howled through the masts and guy ropes and smashed against the bamboo cabin. Luckily, the cabin was tied down and made of springy bamboo walls that bounced with the wind. Wave upon wave surged up and came crashing toward them, but the water washed by harmlessly.

What they'd discovered was that the raft was ideally suited for cutting through heavy seas. Water didn't collect on deck and sink the raft, after all; it just slid through the gaps between the logs.

In fact, if they had built the raft using modern technology, they would have gone to the bottom of the ocean long ago. To everyone's horror, they'd followed the specifications of the ancient Incas, found in the records of the Spanish conquistadors of the 16th century. They hadn't understood how the raft would actually work, but they followed the old diagrams anyway.

Once at sea, they'd discovered how perfect the ancient design really was. The shifting logs didn't snap the ropes, because the wood was softer than the hemp. Instead, the ropes slowly cut into the logs until they were snugly embedded. The lighter, dry logs that everyone had advised them to use would have become waterlogged and sunk. Instead, they'd used green logs, full of sap, which kept the salt water out. Following the diagrams, they'd also implemented an ancient steering method. Between the logs, they wedged in centerboards—long, thin fir planks that went about 1.5 meters (five feet) below the raft. After experimenting, they'd learned that by raising or lowering the planks, the raft would turn this way or that.

They didn't need a motor because the swift Humbolt Current, which swept up the west coast of South America before heading west across the Pacific, carried them along at a steady clip.

After five days the storm died down. By then the *Kon-Tiki* was looking worse for wear. Despite its startling suitability for this kind of voyage, it couldn't last forever. They needed to reach land soon.

AFTER A ROUGH LAUNCH on April 28, 1947, and a few days of struggling with the heavy steering oar, they'd learned how to maneuver the raft. The sail, centerboards, and steering oar enabled

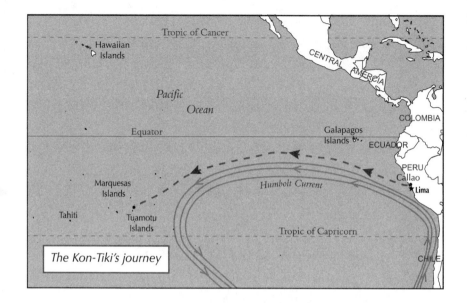

The Kon-Tiki's journey

them to harness the power of the current and trade winds and
to steer reasonably well.

None of the six men was an experienced sailor, but this was
intentional. For their experiment to work, they couldn't have any
modern knowledge of sailing.

Hesselberg had some basic navigation skills, but Danielsson
was a sociologist interested in human migration theories. Both
Haugland and Raaby were radio experts. Watzinger was an engi-
neer and took careful measurements of the weather and ocean.
Once they landed—*if* they landed—this information would be
useful to meteorologists and hydrographical experts, who had
almost no data about the middle of the ocean where ships never
ventured.

Their raft was little more than a floating experiment for the
American navy and the British military. They'd been given the
newest of inventions: the rubber dinghy needed to be tested in
real-life conditions, as did their floating cutlery, stove, splash-proof

sleeping bags, and sunburn cream. Raaby and Danielsson had promised to eat nothing during the voyage but newly devised packaged rations, and to report on whether the canned food contained enough nutrition for survival. The British military wanted them to test a "shark powder" that could be sprinkled in the water to deter aggressive sharks.

So far, six weeks after launching, most things had worked. Raaby and Danielsson, who weren't fond of seafood to begin with, were surviving well on their canned food. Paddling around in the dinghy, they all took off-raft excursions to film the raft or just for fun.

Away from the hustle and worries of daily life, their days were mostly peaceful. Danielsson had brought along 73 scientific books and only had a couple left to finish. Hesselberg filled a sketchbook with scenes from life on board or played his guitar. Heyerdahl kept a daily journal. Instead of testing the shark powder, they'd learned to catch smaller sharks by hand, making a sport out of hanging onto the shark's tail while the ferocious animal thrashed on deck. They also fished for bonitos, tunnies, and dolphin fish.

Not that they were ever short of food. When they woke up in the morning, all they had to do was pick up the flying fish that had landed on deck overnight and cook them. One day, a flying fish struck Haugland's hand as he held the frying pan. With a flick of Haugland's wrist, the fish was on its way to being breakfast.

ON JULY 17, the sight of two large birds flying overhead caused great excitement. These birds, called boobies, were their first visitors from the west, which meant they had to be close to Polynesia. Their enthusiasm was dampened only by the thought that they didn't know how to beach the raft.

There's an old saying about transportation: *Learn to stop before you start.* But Heyerdahl and his crew were learning as they went and had no practice in landing.

As far as they could tell, they were an equal distance from two island groups, the Tuamotus and Marquesas. Without a motor or sophisticated steering, they couldn't travel against the strong current, so they couldn't intentionally aim for either group. They were more or less at the mercy of the current and shifting winds.

They might just float past all the islands in their path, or crash into the rocky volcanic cliffs of the Marquesas. Even if they ended up heading toward the low-lying Tuamotu islands as they hoped, the *Kon-Tiki* could founder on the treacherous reefs hidden under the shallow water.

According to their calculations, they were heading straight toward Fatu Hiva, the very island where Heyerdahl had lived and heard the traditional Polynesian stories. Then without warning and before the island was even in sight, the winds changed, taking them south onto a current that headed for Antarctica. For a couple of days, they contemplated the possibility that they might just float in a never-ending circle around the Pacific. Then their trusty trade wind returned, steering them toward the Tuamotus again. Now at least they were headed in the right direction.

ON JULY 30, they caught their first delicious glimpse of land. They gazed wistfully at the low-lying strip on the horizon, but the strong current pulled them past.

That night, Danielsson complained about not having a chair. Heyerdahl woke in the middle of the night, after dreaming of steak and onions. After three happy months, knowing their journey was almost over made them feel dissatisfied for the first time, impatient for it to end.

Four days later, they spotted land again, but it was surrounded by a ring of sharp coral. Their raft had been sighted, though, and several men paddled out to greet them excitedly. The islanders tried to tow the raft through the one narrow opening in the reef. Even with their help, the current was too strong and the *Kon-Tiki* drifted past the little island.

For the next three days, the crew saw no more glimpses of land. Now they were headed toward the Raroia and Takume atolls. These two ring-shaped dots were part of the Tuamotu Archipelago, a long stretch of tiny islands and treacherous reefs. They would not be a safe place to go ashore. Luckily, they were able to skirt around most of the archipelago and only needed to clear the southernmost tip. They set their course south, and went to sleep at the end of their hundredth day at sea.

HEYERDAHL WOKE IN THE MIDDLE OF THE NIGHT, uneasy. Something in the motion of the raft and the movement of the waves felt different. In the pitch black, he couldn't see a thing, so fell back into a restless sleep.

At dawn, Raaby, who was on watch, shimmied down the mast. A group of small palm-covered islands lay ahead. The wind must have shifted during the night, for these had to be the very islands they'd been trying to avoid. Even if they once again pointed the nose of the raft due south, their drift would carry it into one of them. They soon realized that they would have only a few more hours on board the *Kon-Tiki*: shipwreck was inevitable.

After planning what each man would do when the fateful moment came, they took their positions. Whatever happened, they had to stay on board until the *Kon-Tiki* was grounded. If anyone tried to beat through the crashing waves in the dinghy, he would be torn to shreds by the sharp coral and pounding surf. The heavy balsa logs were their best protection.

Soon the raft was bucking and heaving over the rough seas. The ocean crashed against the invisible but deadly reef, sucking water down, then spitting it out again.

On board, all valuables were stowed in the cabin, wrapped in whatever watertight material the men could find, and lashed down. After covering the cabin with canvas, tying it securely with strong ropes, they fashioned a makeshift anchor and tied their longest rope to it. For the first time in months they put on shoes, in anticipation of clambering over the razor-like coral.

For hours, the ocean pushed them toward their inevitable fate. They threw the anchor overboard to swing the back of the raft toward the breakers. Raaby tapped away at the radio keys inside the cabin, trying to make final contact with Rarotonga, the main island of the Cook Islands, to the southwest. He sent out the coordinates of their position and a message that if Rarotonga didn't hear from them in 36 hours, they were to contact the Norwegian Embassy in Washington, DC to send out a search party. Then he closed down the radio and took up his position on deck. They were ready for whatever would hit them.

The anchor rope was cut when it became obvious that they couldn't resist the tug of the sea. The only plan was to stay on the raft until the waves pushed them close enough to shore. Each man clung as tightly as possible to his rope. A great rush of water lifted the raft high, flinging it forward. "Hooray!" Heyerdahl shouted. But then a second wave rose up behind. The shimmering green wall loomed high overhead, as they sank low in the trough it created. Then it violently pounded down on their backs.

On its heels another wave rose up and flattened them against the balsa logs. Desperately, Heyerdahl hung onto the rope. Water rushed violently all around him, tossing him like a feather in the breeze. The second wave passed, and then a third. Haugland shouted victoriously, "Look at the raft, she's holding!" The cabin and mast were only slightly crooked—they were invincible.

Just then, a fourth wave surged up behind them, as high as a house. After hollering a warning, Heyerdahl curled up into a tight knot. The water hammered down. Horrified, the others saw him disappear under a foaming, furious wall.

As the wave hit the other men, a series of bone-shaking bumps told Heyerdahl they'd hit the reef at last. Water rushed over the raft in a swirling mass. With an unknown strength, Heyerdahl hung on, his only thought that he mustn't let go of the rope.

The ocean thundered past, leaving chaos behind. The mast had snapped like a twig and fallen on the cabin roof. The steering oar was shattered, the deck was torn up, and boxes and cans lay scattered about. Heyerdahl could see only one other survivor: Watzinger. Where were the four others? He shouted and heard Danielsson's voice come from under a pile of matting, "All men aboard!"

A few more punishing waves pushed them into shallower water. Haugland jumped overboard and walked across the reef until he was safely out of reach of the undertow.

Hesselberg and Danielsson crawled out from under the flattened cabin, while Raaby and Watzinger emerged from underneath piles of wreckage. Apart from a slight concussion suffered by Danielsson, they were no worse for wear.

After that, each new wave carried them a little closer to shore. One by one they jumped off, wading shoreward across the wide ring of reef. When they had made it safely past the most dangerous part, they found their waterlogged dinghy and began to salvage the most important items off the wrecked raft. Slowly the tide receded and they could see bright flashes of color in the water at their feet: swirling anemones, darting fish, and glittering shells.

Wherever they were, they'd landed on the shallow reef between two islands: a long forested one and, closer, a smaller one dotted with palms. They chose the smaller one, which looked like the perfect tropical island.

With growing anticipation, they walked through the shallows. It had been more than three months since they'd last set foot on land. They laughed at the novelty of their first footprints, then luxuriated in the cool shade of the palm trees and the heady scent of coconut blossoms. They ran their fingers through the deliciously dry sand, and flopped onto their backs. Watzinger climbed up a small palm and cut down a clutch of green coconuts. With a machete, he lopped off the tops. The crew toasted their miraculous landing with a cool drink of coconut milk. They might not know exactly where they were, but it was paradise.

THOR HEYERDAHL AND THE REST of the *Kon-Tiki* crew had landed on a small, uninhabited island east of Tahiti after 101 days at sea. They christened it Kon-Tiki Island. After a lot of struggle and tense waiting, they were finally able to coax their soggy radio to send out a message confirming their safety. Inhabitants from the neighboring island soon found them and welcomed them. Weeks of celebrations culminated in a day-long feast, then they tearfully said goodbye and boarded a cargo boat for Tahiti. Later, a Norwegian steamer picked them up. Their grand adventure was over.

While it was impossible to prove conclusively that the Polynesians were direct descendants of their mythical hero Tiki, the *Kon-Tiki* expedition did prove that ocean migration could have happened thousands of years ago.

Afterward, Heyerdahl wrote a popular book called *Kon-Tiki*, and a documentary film about his journey won an Academy Award in 1951. He later organized three voyages similar to the *Kon-Tiki* trip, in ancient Egyptian reed boats, continuing his quest to understand ancient peoples. After setting off on expeditions and adventures up until his eighties, Heyerdahl died in 2002 at the age of 87.

Thor Heyerdahl's unorthodox methods and controversial theories still challenge accepted beliefs, though he has his followers, as well as a research center named after him. Regardless of whether his theories are true or not, he is remembered as a daring—and unique—adventurer.

Special Delivery

Virginia to Pennsylvania, March 1849

IT WAS A DANGEROUS PLAN. But as soon as the idea came to him, Henry Brown knew he'd do it: he would ship himself to freedom. The 33-year-old black slave would risk anything to be a free man, even his own life.

As a slave in the American South, Brown knew that his only hope lay in reaching one of the states north of the Ohio River, where slavery had been abolished. A local storekeeper, Samuel Smith, had agreed to help him escape but after wracking their brains for weeks, neither man had come up with a satisfactory plan. In despair, Henry prayed, and while doing so a thought flashed across his mind. He would shut himself up in a wooden box and have himself shipped, like a package of goods, to a free state.

The scheme was so outrageous and daring, it might actually work. Who would suspect a wooden box? And who would think a person could survive such a torturous journey?

Immediately, Brown told Smith, but to the storekeeper the plan sounded like a slow, cruel form of suicide. But Brown was determined, so Smith agreed to accompany the box on its journey north, to ensure that it—with Brown inside—would be treated carefully. He wrote a letter to a friend in Philadelphia, asking for assistance once Brown arrived.

Brown was lucky enough to have a little bit of money saved. Half of this went to Smith for his help. With the rest, he hired a carpenter to build the box: 3 feet 1 inch long, 2 feet wide, and 2½ feet high. These dimensions were small enough to look inconspicuous, and just barely big enough to squeeze in Brown's 91-kilogram (200-pound) body. The box was lined with a thin layer of baize, the same material used to cover billiard tables and all that would protect him from the hard wooden boards. He would first travel by train from Richmond, Virginia to the Potomac River, then by steamship to Washington, and finally by train again to Philadelphia. In all, the trip would take about 27 hours, provided there were no unexpected delays.

Meanwhile, Samuel Smith had heard nothing from his friend in Philadelphia, but he and Brown resolved to carry on anyway, hoping a reply would come before they left.

For the plan to work, Brown needed to buy himself some time. His finger happened to be cut badly, so he showed it to his overseer at the tobacco factory where he worked and asked for a couple of days off to let it heal. "It's not so bad," the overseer said and refused the request.

At that, Brown went to another friend for help, a free black man named Dr. James Smith. Dr. Smith gave him a small vial of sulfuric acid, telling him that a few drops would make the wound look worse. In his haste, Brown spilled too much acid over his finger and soon it had eaten through his flesh to the bone. When he showed the now large, serious wound to the overseer, Brown was told to go home until it got better.

But instead, Brown immediately went to Samuel Smith's store. By this time, the friend in Philadelphia had replied and agreed to pick up the package as soon as it arrived. The two men arranged to meet with Dr. Smith at the store at four o'clock the next morning to be ready for the first express train.

Apart from the clothes he was wearing, Brown brought very little. He filled a small container with water for drinking or to splash on his face if he felt faint. For air, he bored three air holes—too small to be noticed—through the top of the box. He kept the tool with him in case he needed to drill more holes in an emergency.

On March 29, 1849, Brown, Samuel Smith, and James Smith met at the store. With a final goodbye, Brown climbed into the wooden box and crouched down, holding his knees close to his chest. He bowed his head as the other two men nailed down the lid. As agreed, they wrote the Philadelphia address and the message "This side up with care" on the box. Imprisoned in his dark, cramped, coffin-like container, Brown was bound for freedom.

UP UNTIL THE PREVIOUS AUGUST, Henry Brown's life as a slave had been bearable enough. His master, William Barret, didn't beat him and even let him keep a small portion of his wages. Most slaves worked on plantations and spent their days either in the fields or as house servants. They weren't paid, nor did they own anything, but depended on their owners for food, clothes, and shelter. Their owners controlled what they learned (if anything), where they lived, and where they went. Depending on their master's personality, slaves were treated well or poorly. Many were disciplined with beatings or imprisonment, or chained and shackled to prevent escapes.

The more fortunate slaves were trained as tradesmen, such as blacksmiths, carpenters, bricklayers, or tobacconists, as Brown was. His skills were valuable enough that he made more money for his master by working in a tobacco factory than he would have in the fields.

The best part of Brown's life was his wife Nancy and their three children. Nancy was owned by the Cottrells and worked as a maid and washerwoman. Unfortunately, Mr. Cottrell was a harsher man than Brown's master, Mr. Barret.

For the privilege of living together as a family, the Browns paid dearly: Mr. Cottrell had insisted Henry rent a house so that he wouldn't have to bear the cost of sheltering Nancy, then demanded an additional $50 a year, saying, "If you don't do this, I will sell her as soon as I can get a buyer for her." Slaves always feared that at any time their loved ones could be sold to a new master and shipped away. They were considered property, the same as a horse or cow, and owners gave no thought to breaking up families. At that time, many believed slaves had no feelings anyway.

As slaves were not allowed to rent houses, Henry Brown had gone to Dr. James Smith for help. As a free black man, Smith was able to arrange the rental and so the Browns managed to stay on Cottrell's good side for several years. They even considered themselves lucky. As Henry later wrote, "life had joys worth living" as long as he was allowed to be with his family. But with Cottrell as his wife's master, their future would always be uncertain.

One morning in August 1848, Cottrell came to the Browns' house demanding more money. "You know I have no money to spare!" Henry replied. He was, after all, giving his low wages to two owners—his own master Barret, and Cottrell—plus paying for rent and living expenses.

That answer wasn't good enough for Cottrell. "I want money," he said, "and money I will have."

After he left, Henry asked his wife, "I wonder what Mr.

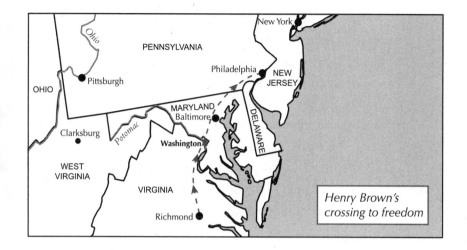

PENNSYLVANIA

Ohio

Pittsburgh

OHIO

New York

Philadelphia

NEW
JERSEY

DELAWARE

MARYLAND
Baltimore

Clarksburg

Potomac

Washington

WEST
VIRGINIA

VIRGINIA

Richmond

Henry Brown's
crossing to freedom

Cottrell means." Nancy burst into tears, saying perhaps he would sell one of their children. With a heavy heart, Henry left for work. Cottrell was up to something.

A few hours later, a man burst into the tobacco factory with the news that Nancy and the children had all been sold at an auction. They were already in jail and would be shipped to another state the next day.

Brown did everything he could to free his wife and children, including begging his own master to buy her. Barret angrily replied, "Mr. Cottrell is a gentleman. I am afraid to meddle with his business," then ordered Brown to leave. In desperation, Brown went to two friends, but they also refused to buy his family back.

The next morning Brown sorrowfully watched as over 300 slaves, with ropes around their necks and hands bound together, were led out of town. He heard his children crying after him, then spotted Nancy. He grabbed her hand and they walked together for as long as possible, though both were too distraught to speak. Finally, Brown was forced to let her go.

With no family to keep him in Richmond and make slavery somewhat bearable, Brown started thinking seriously about escaping. Some slaves escaped on their own and managed to dodge the slave catchers and bloodhounds sent after them. For others, there was the Underground Railroad, a secret network of hiding places and people who helped slaves escape to the northern free states and Canada. For months Brown tried to come up with a plan, but none seemed as if it would actually work. He decided at last that he couldn't escape on his own.

After years of buying goods in Samuel Smith's store, Brown felt that the white man was trustworthy. He also guessed that Smith was secretly an abolitionist, someone who believed in ending slavery, so he took the risk of asking him for help. Brown was right, and Smith agreed to do what he could. But it was Brown himself who finally came up with the best plan.

WITH A BUMP, Henry Brown felt himself land on the floor of the Express Office. Almost immediately, he was tipped on his head while a baggage handler nailed something to the bottom of the crate. Unable to protest, Brown silently endured the discomfort. When he was shifted again, still upside down, he guessed that he was now on the wagon that would take him to the train station. With every bump along the dirt road, a jolt of pain stabbed through Brown's skull and ran down his body. Why hadn't Smith told the baggage handlers to turn his crate over? And why weren't the handlers following the instructions written on top?

At the train station, he was roughly tumbled onto the baggage car but luckily fell on his right side. By then it was apparent that Samuel Smith wasn't accompanying him after all. He would be at the mercy of uncaring baggage handlers and dockworkers, treated like a crate of apples. His already risky journey had just become much more dangerous. Sealed inside and surrounded by people who would more than likely turn him in, there was nothing he could do.

Brown's next stop was the Potomac River, where his crate was heaved up from the baggage car, carried a ways and set down in the steamer's hold—upside down again. Brown wriggled as much as he dared, trying to find the least painful position. Not only were the tiny air holes pressed against the floor again, but the room was hot and stuffy. If he stayed in this position for the entire river journey, he'd run out of air. Blood rushed to his head and he could feel his eyes swelling until he thought they'd burst from their sockets. The veins on his head throbbed. He tried to lift his hand to his head, but couldn't move it. Soon he was covered in a cold sweat, convinced he would die. Brown remained in this unbearable position for what felt like forever, though he later estimated it was an hour and a half.

Just when he could bear it no longer, he heard two men talking. One man said that he'd love to sit down—they'd traveled a long way and had been standing for hours, after all. After tossing Brown's crate onto its side, the two men sat on top. Relieved, Brown lay quietly inside, feeling the blood drain from his head. Cautiously, he drank a sip of water from his container and splashed a little on his face.

"What do you suppose this box contains?" one man said. The other replied that it was probably the mail.

I think it's a male too, Brown thought.

WHEN THE STEAMSHIP LANDED AT WASHINGTON, Brown was again transferred by wagon, though this time, placed right side up. The wagon stopped and from the shouting outside Brown could tell they'd arrived at the train station. The driver called for help with lifting the box and someone replied that he should just throw it off.

The driver pointed out that it was marked "this side up with care," so its contents might be breakable. The other man dismissed this, saying that it didn't matter if everything inside broke, the railroad could afford to pay for it.

With that, Brown felt himself violently tumble to the ground and land on his head. His neck cracked as if it had been snapped in two and he blacked out.

When he came to, someone outside was saying, "There is no room for the box. It will have to remain and be sent through tomorrow with the luggage train." Fearing the worst, and not knowing if he could survive an extra day, Brown started praying. To his relief, he heard another man reply that the box had come with the express, so must be sent on.

He was then tumbled onto the wagon and placed on his head for the third time. He was more battered and bruised than he'd ever been in his life. Fortunately, the wagon hadn't gone far before the luggage was shuffled around to make room for another box. Brown found himself tipped right side up again. Soon he was placed in the train's baggage car. The next stop was Philadelphia.

WHILE SAMUEL SMITH DIDN'T ACCOMPANY Henry Brown to Philadelphia (for reasons that aren't recorded), he did send a telegram to his contact in Philadelphia, James Miller McKim. The message said to expect a package of "dry goods"—the code term among abolitionists for a male slave—on the early morning train. At least Brown wouldn't be left waiting any longer than necessary.

Abolitionists such as Smith and McKim were always at risk and needed to work in secret. While slavery was illegal in many northern states by this time, anyone helping a fugitive slave could still be fined there. In the southern states, they could be sentenced to hard labor in prison.

THE TRAIN HUFFED AND PUFFED as it slowed down, so Brown knew it was approaching a station. By then, he'd been traveling for almost 24 hours. Every muscle was stiff and bruised; even his bones ached. Maybe Samuel Smith had been right and he'd arrive at his destination as a corpse. He wriggled his toes, then wet his lips with some of the last of his water. Tired, hungry, and thirsty, he wondered how much longer he would last in his hard wooden cage.

"We're in Philadelphia," he heard someone cry amongst the bustle of station activity. Joy and hope flooded through him—he'd arrived!

He didn't even care when his box was carelessly dumped in the train station alongside the other packages. But once there, he waited. Minutes ticked away and dragged into hours. After about three hours, he heard a wagon pull up and a voice ask whether a box from Richmond, Virginia had arrived.

As he bounced along the road, Brown could hardly breathe for excitement. He didn't dare make a noise in case the driver wasn't sympathetic to fugitive slaves. To be captured this close to freedom would be unbearable.

The wagon stopped and several men lifted the box, grunting and groaning. Inside, Brown could only guess that he'd finally reached the address written on the top. Once he was placed down, all was silent. Not knowing what was going on, Brown didn't move or make a sound.

After a few minutes of tense waiting, Brown heard a loud knock against the box and a voice cautiously say, "Is all right within?"

"All right," he called out.

His reply astonished everyone and he heard shouts of amazement and joy. They'd obviously expected him to be dead. Anxiously, Brown listened to the sound of the nails being pried out. Fresh air rushed in as the lid lifted. Brown blinked against the light and slowly uncurled from his fetal position. Even so, when he struggled to stand, he fell down in a faint.

When he woke up, he saw four men, one black and the others white, watching him anxiously. On seeing his eyes open, they helped him up and welcomed him to a new life of freedom. Brown felt as if he'd actually risen from the dead. He was too overwhelmed with emotion to know what to say. Instead, he started singing Psalm 40: "I waited patiently for the Lord; And he heard my calling." It was a verse about being delivered from hardship, just as Brown had been, and he sang the words with all his heart.

BROWN DID NOT STAY LONG with his new friends in Philadelphia. Although he was now in a state where slavery was illegal, he could be captured by his master, who still legally owned him. Arrangements were made for Brown to continue on to Massachusetts, then New York, where he stayed with a doctor who cared for his finger—it hadn't yet healed from the sulfuric acid. While there, he heard of an anti-slavery meeting that would

no immunity to it. Entire villages were often wiped out.

The fire was to "clean the air," a common native practice to attempt to stop the spread of the disease. Most of the surviving villagers had fled in the canoes meant for Isabel's party. While they couldn't know for sure, some suspected her father's group may have brought the disease to the village. Ironically, his effort to help may have destroyed their plans.

Things got worse. When Isabel woke the next day, she discovered that the 31 porters had disappeared, undoubtedly scared of the smallpox.

Some of the party wanted to go back, but they were over-ruled. They'd never be able to cross the mountains without porters. Isabel convinced the two villagers to build a canoe and guide them downriver to Andoas. They spent two weeks building a cedar canoe large enough for ten passengers and two crew.

While they waited, the party got their first real experience of the jungle. During the day, they could marvel at the profusion of life. But at night, the forest felt frightening, even sinister. In those days, the Amazon was a place of mythical proportions and dangers. Early explorers published terrifying reports of ferocious Amazon women and a hostile tribe of headless men with eyes in their shoulders and mouths on their chests. Frogs and toads rained from the sky and vampire bats crept into tents to suck the blood from their victims' faces. Even though they had been born in South America, Isabel and her companions likely believed these fantastical tales. The dangers they actually faced were challenging enough, but those they imagined filled them with terror.

When the canoe was ready, they were relieved. Reduced from three canoes to one, they were forced to leave most of the valuable cargo behind, but at least they were alive and hoped to reach Andoas in two weeks.

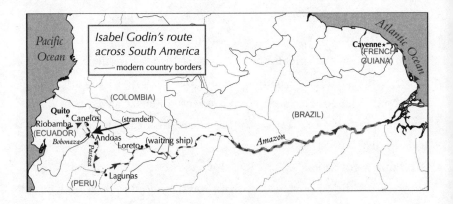

Isabel Godin's route across South America
— modern country borders

Pacific Ocean

Atlantic Ocean

Cayenne ★ (FRENCH GUIANA)

(COLOMBIA)

(BRAZIL)

Quito ★
Riobamba ★ Canelos ★ (stranded)
(ECUADOR)
Bobonaza ★ Andoas ★ (waiting ship)
Pastaza ★ Loreto ★
Amazon

★ Lagunas
(PERU)

For two days, the villagers expertly piloted the canoe through narrow gorges and rushing rapids. In the evenings, they built shelters and caught food for the meals. But when the 10 travelers woke on the third morning after leaving Canelos, their guides had disappeared. Paying them in advance, Isabel realized, had been a grave mistake. They had left the canoe—unfortunately, no one had experience with canoes and most couldn't even swim.

"The only way we can go is forward," Isabel said. They all nodded. "Joaquín, you can steer," she said.

"I'll navigate," volunteered the doctor, Rocha.

Juan and Antonio sat in the middle, paddling as best they could. The others watched for obstacles, kept their belongings from falling overboard, and bailed out water that sloshed over the sides.

At noon the following day, they spotted a canoe on a beach up ahead. They scrambled to shore. A path led to a hut and to their relief they found a native man recovering from smallpox. Although he was still weak, Isabel convinced him to guide them down the river and he even seemed happy to help.

They continued peacefully for two days. They'd reached a flat swampy flood plain where the Bobonaza River twisted, turned, and doubled back on itself. It was October 30, nearly a month after they'd left, and they were only about halfway between Canelos and Andoas.

On October 31, their good luck floated away.

As they drifted along, a gust of wind blew Rocha's hat into the water. Their native guide, who'd been steering, reached over to catch it and fell into the water. He struggled weakly and, before they could help him, drowned. At first they were too stunned to react. Then Joaquín carefully made his way to the rear of the boat to take over the steering.

But the canoe turned sideways in the current, hit a log and tipped over, tossing them into the river. Panic-stricken, they grabbed for the boat and, after much difficulty, pushed it to shore. Luckily, everyone survived.

Most of their supplies were recovered, and they built a makeshift shelter, but their situation was desperate. After the near drowning, Isabel and her two brothers refused to get back in the canoe. For two days, they sat on the beach.

On the third day, Rocha proposed a solution. "I will continue downstream to Andoas," he said. He, his companion Bogé, and Joaquín would take the canoe. Without so much weight, steering would be easier. They were sure to reach Andoas in five or six days. After gathering a crew, they would paddle upstream to rescue those left behind. With no other options, Isabel agreed. On the morning of November 3, Rocha, Bogé, and Joaquín set off.

As they disappeared around the bend, Isabel felt uneasy. They were now stranded in the jungle. And as she searched through the cargo, she realized that not only had Rocha been careful to pack all of his belongings, but also her jewelry box.

THERE WAS NOTHING TO DO BUT SIT AND WAIT. Hours dragged on into days.

It was a tortuous time. The thick humid air and heat sapped their strength and hurt their throats. Surrounded by swampland, they were now food for millions of insects. Soon they were covered in itchy bites that blossomed into sores.

On the 25th day by their reckoning (though each day blurred into the next), they gave up hope of rescue. With their food supplies nearly gone, they had to leave. Using a machete, they cut down a few trees and vines and made a small, fragile raft.

There wasn't room for all of them, so only Isabel, her brothers and nephew pushed off, leaving the young maids with Rocha's slave. Before long the current grabbed the unsteady craft and spun it around. The branch of a sunken tree snagged the raft and in a flash, it flipped. Once again, they were pitched into the muddy river.

Isabel gasped for air, but her sodden dress and petticoats weighed her down. A hand grabbed her dress, pulling her up. She took a breath, then sank once again. Another hand grabbed her and dragged her toward the bank. Her brothers had saved her life. Wet and discouraged, they trudged back to the beach.

They were now even worse off. They hadn't drowned, but had lost their precious provisions and the raft. They would have to continue on foot along the river's edge.

First, Isabel had to get rid of her dress. It was too awkward to walk in and besides, had almost drowned her. She put on a spare pair of her brother's pants. Everyone was alarmed at the sight of a lady in pants, but Isabel felt much freer. With a surge of determination, she stepped into the gloom of the jungle.

LOOKING AT A MAP, the lower Bobonaza scribbles back and forth crazily. Following its banks is not only the longest distance between any two points, but hard going too. Thick undergrowth, trees, and vines have to be hacked away at every turn. The travelers were already weak, so progress was slow. They soon decided to head inland, hoping for an easier, more direct route.

Earlier travelers had described the jungle as a "green hell." The leafy canopy high above them stole most of the light and rainwater. Brilliant blossoms, juicy fruit, and rich nuts swung from the uppermost branches of the trees, far out of reach. Every once in a while, they'd spot a palm cabbage and descend on it ravenously. They drank when they found a stream, but often walked for long hours without water.

By this point, they had no plan, no map, and no idea where Andoas was. Each day, they walked until heat and exhaustion forced them to stop. At dusk, the insects came out in full force, barely letting up throughout the night. They were soon plagued with botfly larvae. These pests burrowed under their skin and grew into fat little worms, causing great discomfort.

They stumbled on, growing constantly weaker. Finally, they collapsed at the foot of a tree and waited for death.

JOAQUÍN DID RETURN TO THE SANDBAR where the group had been stranded. After safely reaching Andoas, Rocha and Bogé had lost interest in returning for the others. Joaquín gathered a crew of natives and set off. Paddling upriver, however, took twice as long as floating downriver.

When he arrived at the sandbar, Joaquín found a grisly scene: no one was in the shelter, but clothing and the straw beds lay scattered around. In the forest, he found a pile of bones, picked clean. Part of a cadaver lay in a river eddy. *What had happened?* Something from the forest had attacked, but there were not enough bones for seven bodies. And there were signs that at least one person had headed into the jungle.

For four days, Joaquín and his crew searched the area, but found nothing. If anyone had gone into the forest, they would be dead by now. He returned to Andoas with the sad news: Isabel and the others were dead.

After reporting to the priest there, he was told to deliver the news to Lagunas, the closest mission downriver, with a letter from Rocha and Bogé stating that Isabel had requested his card of liberty. But he was not granted freedom.

After many months, he made his way back to Quito. Through a series of misunderstandings, he was thrown into jail, accused of being responsible for the death of his mistress.

DEEP IN THE JUNGLE by the lower Bobonaza River, Isabel held her young nephew Martín as he breathed his last breath. Over the next couple of days Martín's father, Antonio, and Juan also died.

Isabel closed her eyes and waited to join them, begging God to release her from agony. Weak, delirious, and tormented with thirst, she slipped in and out of consciousness. Meanwhile, industrious insects descended on the corpses.

But inexplicably, Isabel didn't die. After two or three days, she woke suddenly and envisioned her husband's face. She staggered to her feet.

Looking down, she saw that her blouse and shoes had nearly rotted off her. She took one of the shawls they'd been carrying and wrapped it tightly around her top, then picked up the machete. She needed shoes, so she took the pair off Antonio's feet and fashioned them into a pair of sandals.

Weakly, she stumbled through the jungle. On the second day, she found a stream and on the third, a nest of eggs. After not eating for so long, her throat was constricted, and she could barely swallow. As the days passed, she found just enough food to stay alive. At night she shivered despite the heat, the horrifying scene that she'd left behind flickering against her closed eyelids.

On what she counted as her eighth day alone, she came to a river—the Bobonaza, surely. She collapsed on the sandbar and fell asleep. At dawn, the sound of voices woke her. Two native couples were pushing their canoes into the water. She called out weakly, "Will you take me to Andoas?"

To the natives, Isabel appeared like a ghost. A grubby pair of men's pants hung from her gaunt frame and her hair—now completely white—was matted and dirty. When they gave her meat, she couldn't eat it. The women made a broth and carefully fed her.

These four were traveling to Andoas themselves, but stayed on the beach for days to nurse Isabel. They made balms and poultices for her scratches and painstakingly dug out the botfly larvae burrowed in her head. When she was strong enough to travel, they set off downriver.

On reaching Andoas, Isabel climbed out of the canoe, but no one could believe it was her. News of her death had reached the village two months earlier. Isabel wanted to thank her kind rescuers, but had nothing to offer except for her gold chains, so she gave one to each couple. The village priest, however, took the chains away and gave them a piece of coarse cloth instead.

The next day, Isabel requested a canoe and seven natives to take her to Lagunas immediately. Stunned by her determination, the priest agreed. Before she departed, one of the village women gave her a white cotton dress that she'd made during the night.

It took them just eight days to reach Lagunas. By the time they arrived, Isabel's health had worsened so she stayed there six weeks to recover.

She learned that Joaquín, Rocha, and Bogé had reached Andoas, but no one knew their whereabouts. To her shock Rocha showed up in Lagunas. He gave back a few of her jewelry pieces, claiming the rest were destroyed.

Isabel was furious at this man who'd abandoned her family. "It is impossible that I can ever forget that I owe all my misfortunes and all my losses to you," she said, then told him to go away forever.

The village priest in Lagunas sent word downriver that Isabel was alive, and tried to convince her to return home. "You are still at the beginning of a long and tedious voyage," he said. But she insisted. Her companions had perished, she explained, but God had saved her, protecting her from countless perils. She firmly believed that to turn back would be a sin and a waste of the efforts of her native rescuers.

Very well, the priest replied, but she'd need a chaperone: Rocha. Besides, boats traveling downriver were rare, so Rocha would be stranded otherwise. Isabel reluctantly agreed. They set off for Loreto, but she kept as far away from Rocha as was possible in a canoe.

Despite the priest's concerns, they had now reached the tamer part of the Amazon, with regular Spanish settlements along the shore. As news of her imminent arrival spread, villages sent canoes laden with refreshments and provisions to meet her. In one village, she paused long enough to write to officials back in Riobamba, requesting again that Joaquín, wherever he was, be freed.

In Loreto, she and her father reunited tearfully. Don Pedro had always planned on returning to Riobamba once Isabel arrived. Years earlier, his wife had passed away, and now he'd lost two sons and a grandson. He couldn't bear to think of any further harm coming to his daughter, so he decided to stay with her.

The captain of the waiting boat and his 30 oarsmen had arrived in Loreto almost four years earlier. Their relief at finally being able to carry out their orders must have been enormous.

It took about 10 weeks to sail from Loreto to the mouth of the Amazon. Before reuniting with her husband, Jean, Isabel encountered one last hurdle. As the boat entered the Atlantic Ocean, one of its anchors was lost. The captain decided it would be too dangerous to continue, so he moored in a bay to wait for repairs. On hearing that his wife was so near, Jean sailed down the coast to meet her.

Understandably, Isabel was nervous about meeting her husband. She was 20 years older than when he'd last seen her, painfully thin, with white hair, and her face permanently scarred by the botflies.

But when Jean climbed onto the deck of the ship, Isabel realized her fears were unfounded, and they embraced joyfully.

AFTER THREE YEARS IN FRENCH GUIANA, Isabel, Jean, and Don Pedro sailed for France on April 21, 1773. Meanwhile, Joaquín had been released from jail and Isabel's sister arranged for his long-promised freedom.

In France, they settled in Jean's family home and made a comfortable life. Despite her childhood dreams of the salons and high society balls of France, however, Isabel was too self-conscious about her scarred face, and haunted by her losses, to socialize much. She developed a facial tic whenever the subject of the Amazon came up.

In a small ebony box lay the sandals she'd fashioned out of her brother's shoes and the handmade white cotton dress from the native woman in Andoas. After Isabel's death, the ebony box was handed down through generations until it mysteriously disappeared after a family dispute.

The Dead Man's March

Central Africa to Zanzibar, May 1873 to February 1874

IN THE EARLY 1870S, Europe became very interested in Africa. Not only did the riches of Asia lie on the other side, but Africa itself was potentially full of resources. To all but a handful of daring Europeans, the continent and its people were completely unknown and strangely mysterious.

Dr. David Livingstone was probably Europe's best-known explorer. He was famous for his long treks into Africa's interior, contributions to mapmaking, pious Christianity, and campaign to abolish slavery. But his greatest journey—the one told and retold, that inspired millions of English men and women—was made after he died.

AS DAWN BROKE, the caravan leaders gathered around the camp-fire. In spite of the bright sunshine, the men's faces were grim. After seven years of exploring Africa's unmapped interior, the leader of their expedition, David Livingstone, had died only hours before.

"He is gone," said Majwara, the boy who had kept watch throughout the night.

Abdullah Susi, the last person to talk to Livingstone, broke the news. The others, including James Chuma and Jacob Wainwright, hung their heads in both grief and consternation.

Now they had no leader. Worse, they were a long way from anywhere remotely close to "home." Most of the expedition's 70 or more men and women had either come from Zanzibar island on the east coast (the unofficial starting point for most European-led expeditions into Africa) or along the way. They worked as porters, cooks, scouts, interpreters, and guides, came from a variety of tribes (sometimes warring ones), and spoke a mix of languages. Many were freed slaves.

The closest village to their encampment, ruled by Chief Chitambo, lay south of Lake Bangweulu (in what is now northern Zambia) in Africa's interior. Between the village and Zanzibar lay the eastern half of Africa—a journey of roughly 2200 kilometers (nearly 1400 miles). It was the battleground for wars between African rulers, and the source for a booming slave trade. Livingstone had hated seeing the men, women, and children chained together in long lines, being marched away from their homes.

The purpose of Livingstone's exploration had been to discover the source of the Nile. At the time, a debate was raging across Europe about the origin of the world's longest river. Several expeditions had been launched by other explorers, but nothing had been confirmed. Livingstone believed that the Nile began somewhere near the headwaters of the Luapula (in what is now Zambia) or Lualaba (in Congo) rivers, which would feed into the Nile.

In 1866, Livingstone was 53 years old, an age when most men were ready to settle comfortably into retirement. But instead, he'd set off on what became his last expedition. After years of fruitless exploration, shortly after his 60th birthday, the explorer was finally stopped by the many ailments that had plagued him for months: dysentery, fever, hemorrhoidal bleeding, and mysterious back pain. When he couldn't go any farther, he lay down in a hastily made grass hut outside Chitambo's village. Days later, he quietly passed away.

Now the party's head men, including James Chuma, Abdullah Susi, Manua Sera, Chowpereh, and Jacob Wainwright, had to decide what to do with the explorer's body and the papers that were so important to him.

The easiest solution would be to hastily bury the body and leave. Yet they all agreed on what to do: carry Livingstone's body back to Zanzibar, where it could then be shipped home to Great Britain. They also agreed to keep the death a secret from Chief Chitambo, who had allowed them to set up camp just outside his village. The chief would likely be furious that they had brought death into his midst.

Most of these men were already experienced trekkers. Between them, they had been on every significant expedition in Africa in the past 15 years, in an age of frantic exploration and mapmaking. Despite their experience and skills in navigation, diplomacy, and languages, they were worried. Most tribes had taboos and fears associated with dead bodies. They would resent strangers carrying a dead man through their villages and would either drive them out or charge expensive *hongos,* or tolls, before letting them pass. The only thing in their favor was that the rainy season—constant showers, miserable cold—was over.

First they had to remove Livingstone's body from the grass hut. Following custom, they carried the body out, not through the front door, but through a hole broken in the back wall. Then, sending word that Livingstone was simply too sick to receive visitors, they moved camp a little farther from the village. There they built a roofless enclosure of reeds around the body.

It was too big a secret to be kept long. The next day, Chitambo heard the news. To their relief, he wasn't angry. When Susi heard of the chief's reaction, he took him a gift and confirmed the rumor. Chitambo replied, "Now my people shall mourn." At this, the villagers began weeping and shouting in the traditional way.

The expedition party fired volleys from their guns in tribute. Then they turned to the tricky task of transporting Livingstone's body. They would encounter rough terrain, travel for months through equatorial heat, and pass hungry predators, so the body had to be completely preserved.

One of the men, Farijallah, had worked in a surgeon's house and had watched postmortems, so he was appointed undertaker. He asked another, Carus Farrar, to assist. Susi, Chuma, and Manua Sera held up a thick blanket for privacy while the two men worked.

Farijallah made a single incision in Livingstone's abdomen. Through this small opening, he removed Livingstone's heart, lungs, and abdominal organs and put them into a tin box that had once held the man's journals. From the intestine, he pulled out a massive blood clot the size of a fist—no doubt the cause of Livingstone's severe back pain.

Jacob Wainwright, who could read and write, made notes of their findings in Livingstone's journal, with a detailed inventory of all his belongings. Meanwhile, Farijallah salted Livingstone's empty chest cavity and rubbed brandy over his mouth and scalp. Wainwright then read the burial service from a prayer book, while the small group stood under a tall *mpundu* tree, its high canopy of leaves creating a pool of shade. They stood solemnly as the tin box containing Livingstone's organs was buried.

Their next task was to stop the corpse from decomposing. For the next two weeks, the body was left in its reed enclosure, exposed to the fierce African sun. Guarded day and night against hyenas, it was soon dry as leather. The mummified body was then packaged. Livingstone's knees were bent toward his chest to shorten the body. Then he was wrapped in blue and white striped cotton, and placed in a cylinder of bark. Sailcloth was sewn around the cylinder and the whole package slung from a pole. This way, it could be carried between two men, each balancing the pole over a shoulder.

As a final memorial, Wainwright carved an inscription on the *mpundu* tree. "Livingstone, May 4, 1873," it read, with the names of the three main caravan leaders, Abdullah Susi, Manua Sera, and Chowpereh.

Ready at last, the party set off, but after only a day the body smelled so foul that no one could eat. They sent a few men back to Chitambo's village for a cask of tar that they'd brought with them earlier, intended for Livingstone's boat. They used the tar to cover the bark roll before continuing.

Beyond the swamps that surrounded Lake Bangweulu, rivers snaked through the open grassland. As they trekked, the bare trunks of trees rose up high above their heads before spreading out in a bowl of leaves and twisted branches. In the distance, rocky hills lined the horizon. The plains were alive with herds of impala, zebra, leaping gazelles, and lumbering wildebeest. Scattered among antelope herds, troops of baboons made mischief, while lions prowled silently through the tall grass. Human settlements ranged from small collections of grass shelters to sprawling villages of round, mud-walled huts.

Not only Livingstone's body had to travel in disguise, so did the whole party. Apart from the rare exploration expedition, such

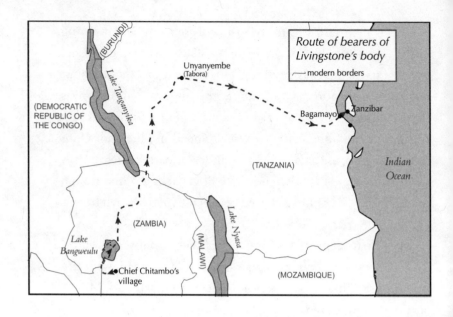

Route of bearers of
Livingstone's body
—— modern borders

as Livingstone's had been, three kinds of travelers roamed the region: invading enemies, slave raiders, or trade caravans.

The group deliberately made themselves look like an important trade caravan. The young boy, Majwara, led the way, beating his drum as he walked. Behind him two men carried flags, England's Union Jack and the red banner of the sultan of Zanzibar. Porters were loaded down with supplies, including Livingstone's journals, papers, equipment, and personal belongings. Their secret cargo was concealed in the middle of the procession, looking like an innocent bundle of trade goods. *We're just traders*, their appearance proclaimed. *There's no dead body in* this *caravan, no sir.*

Chuma, Susi, and Chowpereh also made sure that everyone was pulling his weight. No one was allowed to dawdle. "Ho! You man!" Chuma might holler, grabbing a reluctant porter by the ear or the throat. *"Haya! Haya!"* he'd say in Swahili, the trade language of the area. "Get a move on!"

Although he wasn't especially tall or muscular, the young,

energetic Chuma would fearlessly berate workers twice his size until they grudgingly shouldered their load. A former slave, Chuma had been rescued by English missionaries and later recruited by Livingstone. He loved expedition life and became known for his lively wit and tall tales. He deferred to Susi, however, who was about 20 years older. Despite his weakness for *pombe,* the local beer, Susi had a reputation for being loyal and responsible.

These caravan leaders would have to guide a sometimes unruly and mutinous crew past every obstacle on the long journey.

AFTER ONLY TWO DAYS, they were forced to stop. A mysterious illness had swept through the party, one that caused stabbing facial pain and paralyzed limbs. Chuma couldn't walk, while Susi's pain alternated from leg to leg. They were laid up in a village for an entire month, and two women died.

Another time, a misunderstanding with villagers led to a fight. By the end of the skirmish, they'd set fire to two villages and the locals had fled. Even for peaceful travelers, conflicts were unavoidable. As they continued, they were struck down by illness again, and bad weather.

But after months on the road, they began to pass through territory they'd traveled years earlier with Livingstone. Many villages were now deserted because of fighting in the area, so they set up camp in ghost villages for the night.

After minor hostilities, they reached the long thin Lake Tanganyika, which straddles the border of what is now Congo and Tanzania. A few members of the party had been lost through fighting, sickness, or because they'd run away, tired of the danger and arduous trekking.

By the time they'd reached about halfway up Lake Tanganyika, they'd traveled roughly 1000 kilometers (over 600 miles). But their journey was only half done. They still had nearly 1100 kilometers (675 miles) to go, east to Bagamoyo, a port facing the island of Zanzibar. Their next stop would be Unyanyembe (now Tabora), a major trading center. Initially, the area teemed with game—giraffe, zebra, Cape buffalo and lions. The few marksmen of the party shot enough buffalo not only for themselves, but also as gifts for friendly locals.

In October 1873, five months after leaving Chitambo's village, the group was near Unyanyembe. By then, their good fortune was over, with game animals scarce and their provisions dangerously low. Far ahead, they saw a large caravan that turned out to be a group of friendly Arab traders, who gave the news that an expedition had been sent from England to find Livingstone. It was in Unyanyembe at that very moment.

Their problems appeared to be over; Livingstone's own countrymen were nearby. Jacob Wainwright wrote a letter to the expedition's leader. Chuma and three others ran ahead to deliver it. It notified the Englishman of Livingstone's death, adding, "but we have carried the corpse with us." Wainwright also included a plea: "Ten of our soldiers are lost and some have died. Our hunger presses us to ask you for some clothes to buy provision for our soldiers…." In the interior, money had little value, so cloth and beads were traded for food.

When he read the letter, Lieutenant Lovett Cameron, leader of the Livingstone East-Coast Aid Expedition, could hardly believe that Livingstone was really dead.

His party was not the first that had been sent out to "rescue" Livingstone. Years earlier, an American journalist, Henry Morton Stanley, had been sent by the *New York Herald* to find Livingstone and snag the news scoop of the decade. Their meeting on the coast of Lake Tangyanika would later become famous. According to Stanley, he greeted the explorer by saying, "Dr. Livingstone, I presume?" as if they weren't the only two white men for hundreds of miles.

By the time they reached Unyanyembe, the Livingstone East-Coast Aid Expedition had suffered tragedy as well as the usual trials of travel in Africa. One of the leaders, Livingstone's nephew, had died of malaria. Another, W.E. Dillon, was seriously ill with fever and dysentery. They had been in Unyanyembe since August, wondering whether to continue. But then Wainwright's letter arrived. They gave Chuma supplies to take back. Then, while they debated whether the letter's news was true or not, Livingstone's body was delivered to them.

Livingstone's party entered Unyanyembe with great pomp and ceremony, dressed in their best clothes and decked out with ostrich feathers. But when the two parties met—one African-led, one European-led—sparks flew.

Cameron immediately assumed leadership of both parties and demanded that the corpse be buried right away. Chuma, after consulting with Susi, refused. They insisted on carrying out their original mission, to return Livingstone to his homeland. Cameron shouted angrily, but the men were adamant. The lieutenant was forced to back down.

After resting for a few days, the travel-weary group shouldered their unusual cargo once again and continued east. Two men from Cameron's party joined them: the sick W.E. Dillon and another Englishman, Cecil Murphy, who'd had enough of African travel. Cameron continued westward to collect papers that Livingstone had stored years before in a village farther inland.

The two new members introduced tension to the party. Like

Cameron, Murphy tried to assume the role of leader, but the African caravan leaders were unwilling to relinquish authority. Every detail caused disagreements, but somehow the group trudged forward. Meanwhile, news of their mission traveled ahead, all the way to Bagamoyo on the coast.

When they reached the village of Kasakera a few days later, the local tribesmen refused to let them pass through with the corpse. So close to their final destination, they were finally meeting the kind of opposition they'd feared from the start. Determined to stick to their original plan, they concocted a new bluff.

They sent a letter announcing that they were taking the body back to Unyanyembe for burial. Then they took the body out of its wooden shell and sheathed it with fresh bark, snugly wrapped in cloth. Now it resembled a modest roll of cotton. They filled the original shell with bundles of grass.

Six men set off the way they'd come with the dummy, acting like a funeral procession. As soon as it was dark, the men hid in the jungle. They broke up the fake package and scattered the remnants throughout the dense brush. Then they stealthily rejoined the original party and continued on. The ploy was successful and they passed through Kasakera peacefully.

Their troubles, though, were far from over. Not long after Kasakera, Dillon's illness grew so severe that it drove him insane. Delirious with fever, almost blind, and suffering from acute dysentery, he put a gun to his head and shot himself in front of Chuma and Susi.

After hearing this disturbing news, Cameron backtracked and rejoined them briefly. Secretly, he gave Murphy a letter that declared Murphy's authority over the party. "I place no confidence whatever in Susi," it said, "in fact if rumors are true which have reached me about him, he is an arrant rogue." Murphy was to give this letter to authorities in Zanzibar.

The African caravan leaders were unaware of the letter's existence. In the first week of February 1874, nine months after leaving Chief Chitambo's village, they reached the east coast of Africa. *"Heria bahari!"* or "Welcome sea!" they cried as they approached Bagamoyo.

Despite their triumphant cheers, the party was destitute, their supplies completely exhausted. Since Chitambo's village, they had traveled 2250 kilometers (1400 miles) and had lost 10 men and women. Even so, 79 people, plus Livingstone's body, papers, and belongings, had completed the extraordinary journey.

A group of French priests transferred Livingstone's mummified body to a zinc container inside a wooden coffin. The acting British consul came from Zanzibar to take charge. He paid the men the exact amount of wages they were due, then dismissed them. While we'll never know what happened, Cameron's letter may have convinced the English authorities that the African caravan leaders were disreputable and their contributions to the expedition minor.

Many in the party, including Chuma and Susi, had traveled with Livingstone for seven years or more. But within days, the African expedition had dispersed.

The English assumed that Jacob Wainwright was the leader of the African contingent, presumably because he was literate and spoke English well. Livingstone's body was sent back to England on the next mail boat, with Wainwright aboard, guarding the coffin.

UPON ARRIVING IN ENGLAND, the coffin was carried through streets crowded with mourners. Guns were fired and church bells rang. Livingstone's English funeral took place on April 18, 1874, a couple of weeks short of a full year after his death. Wainwright was one of the eight pallbearers, the only one who had witnessed the original funeral under the *mpundu* tree.

The efforts of Livingstone's party did not go completely unnoticed. The Royal Geographic Society made silver medals to commemorate their deeds, inscribed with each recipient's name. By the time the medals reached Zanzibar, however, most of the intended recipients were long gone.

In the end, Chuma and Susi went down in history as Livingstone's greatest African companions. They were brought to England a few weeks after the funeral by an old friend of Livingstone's, as a thank you. The editor of Livingstone's journals interviewed the men extensively, and so they featured prominently in the record of Livingstone's last adventure. The transport of his body became known as "Livingstone's greatest journey," and the heroic efforts of Chuma and Susi gained mythological status among the English.

As for Livingstone's theory on the source of the Nile, it proved to be wrong, yet led to what many consider his greatest discovery. Lieutenant Cameron, using Livingstone's maps and notes, followed the Lualaba to the mighty Congo River and all the way to the Atlantic. Livingstone left another valuable legacy—detailed observations of a landscape and civilization that would quickly change, and in some cases vanish completely, with the coming of the Europeans.

Into the Frozen Unknown

Northern Rupert's Land (present-day Canada), 1770–1772

SNOW FLEW THICKLY around Samuel Hearne. Under his thin summer clothing, he shivered. So far, nothing on this assignment was going right. The 25-year-old was supposed to be traveling from Prince of Wales Fort on the western shore of Hudson Bay (near today's Churchill, Manitoba) to an unknown river known as either the Far-Off Metal River or the Coppermine. Instead, he was lost, cold, and his guide had just disappeared.

The Hudson's Bay Company, which built Prince of Wales Fort as a fur-trading post, had hired him to find a huge copper mine near where the river emptied into the Arctic Ocean. Native people had brought back lumps of copper from the mine, and now the company wanted to fully exploit the deposit.

Samuel Hearne was one of the few Englishmen braving this new territory. At the time Hearne was hired, the Company wanted to expand its trade west of Hudson Bay and needed to forge alliances with the Dene people who lived there.

Problem was, the Hudson's Bay Company had little idea what the people, climate, and terrain were like. And no one knew how incredibly vast the region was. The Company sent out explorers to map the area, men—like Samuel Hearne—who were fearless or foolish enough to venture into truly unknown lands.

On that day, Hearne probably felt he fell into the "foolish" category. There was no way he would find the Coppermine without the help of the locals, the Chipewyan Dene. A reliable Dene guide would not only know how to survive in the demanding climate, but also the dialects and customs of people they would meet along the way.

A former sailor in the British navy, young Hearne really was a fish out of water. He'd eagerly taken on the job in the hopes of making a name for himself in the Company, and maybe even going down in history. Now, after seven months on the trail, it seemed more likely that he'd go down in a snowdrift and either starve or freeze to death.

He and his party of native companions had managed fairly well until a few days earlier when a gust of wind smashed Hearne's navigational instrument against the rocks. Without his quadrant, he couldn't map his journey, so there was no point in continuing. To Hearne's great shame, they were now returning to the fort; it would take them two or even three months to get there.

A Dene guide, Conne-e-quese, had been hired to guide Hearne, but he was losing patience with the Englishman's helplessness and became less cooperative each day. The two Cree men in the party were no help either. The Company had hired them to assist Hearne, ignoring the fact that the Cree were enemies of the Dene. They also came from the south, east of Hudson Bay and, like Hearne, were unprepared for the northern Barren Lands.

When preparing for the trip, Hearne had known it would take a year, maybe even two or more, so he'd packed as lightly as possible. As the seasons changed, they'd have to make or barter for such provisions as winter clothing, snowshoes, sleds, or canoes. He and the two Cree had hunted and skinned several animals for

Route of bearers of
Livingstone's body
— modern borders

(BURUNDI)

Lake Tanganyika

Unyanyembe
(Tabora)

(DEMOCRATIC
REPUBLIC OF
THE CONGO)

Bagamayo   Zanzibar

(TANZANIA)

Indian
Ocean

(ZAMBIA)

Lake Nyasa

(MALAWI)

Lake
Bangweulu

Chief Chitambo's
village

winter clothing. But the Cree men didn't know how to sew the skins into clothes—that was women's work. Their Dene companions refused to help, and in the mostly treeless Barrens it was next to impossible to find branches to make snowshoes.

So on that day, while Hearne and the two Cree waded through thick snow, Conne-e-quese and the other Dene made quick progress and soon disappeared in the cloud of swirling snow. The three men were on their own.

Just as Hearne was giving up hope, a tall figure emerged out of the white haze. Hearne blinked. Only one man who knew his way around this wilderness was that tall: the Chipewyan Dene leader, Matonabbee. Maybe Hearne wouldn't die that day after all.

MATONABBEE AND HIS SMALL GROUP of fellow Dene were on their way to Prince of Wales Fort when they spotted three clumsy foreigners floundering through the snowdrifts. In a mixture of Cree and English, he asked the shivering white man how he came to be in this remote part of the Barrens, and in such a sorry state, then offered him a warm otter-fur suit. The Cree men looked familiar to him from his visits to the fort, so he told his wives to take the strangers' heavy furs and make two winter outfits.

Matonabbee figured Conne-e-quese must have been intending to teach these naive foreigners a valuable lesson. Chipewyan Dene were proud of their independence and scornful of anyone who couldn't take care of himself. To them, it was plain stupidity for a man to travel far without bringing his own women to cook and make clothing and snowshoes. Conne-e-quese's companions had no reason to ask their wives to work for another man.

But Matonabbee was familiar with European men and their strange ways. He was, in fact, a cross-cultural diplomat of the north. At 15, he had been hired by one of the fort's governors to hunt, along with some Cree. He'd learned a little English and some Cree. As a young man, he'd ventured into the territory of the Athabasca Cree and had negotiated a lasting peace between leaders in several communities.

Matonabbee's party spent a few days walking with the foreigners. After a successful hunt, he treated his guests to a feast, complete with singing and dancing. The next day, he invited Hearne into his tent. The two men shared a *calumet*, or peace pipe, and in a mixture of English, Cree, and Athapaskan, spoke frankly. Matonabbee explained why Hearne's trip had failed. He pointed out the obvious errors, explaining that Hearne needed to travel like a local or he'd never survive.

Matonabbee also promised that, once he had attended to his own business and arrived at the fort, he himself would take Hearne to the far-off river, the Coppermine. After ensuring Hearne was properly outfitted and knew his way, Matonabbee said goodbye.

ONCE HE WAS SAFELY BACK at Prince of Wales Fort, Samuel Hearne met with Governor Moses Norton to give his report. Swallowing his pride, he emphasized the positive outcomes of the unsuccessful journey. He'd gained valuable knowledge about how to travel through the rough terrain. And Matonabbee, a highly respected man, had agreed to lead a third expedition. Hearne volunteered to try once more, despite the hardships. Conditions would be fierce: most of the journey would be north of the treeline, so wood for tent poles, snowshoes, or canoes would be scarce. Game was limited, and the winter would be long and cold.

On December 7, not even two weeks after Matonabbee's arrival at the fort, the two men set off into the wilderness again, accompanied by a small group of Dene. Matonabbee had provided a map (which later proved to be remarkably accurate), but Hearne had no way of knowing just how far away the river really was. In fact, a straight line from the fort to the mouth of the Coppermine River would be close to 1400 kilometres (900 miles)—and they would not travel a direct route.

FROM THE START, Matonabbee treated Hearne as if he'd been adopted into his band. Most Europeans thought the indigenous people belonged to large tribes, but the reality was more complicated. The native people organized themselves into small, mostly independent groups or bands, usually made up of extended family. A Dene group might range from 30 to 140 people, with 6 to 30 hunters. In the north, the scarcity of food meant that these groups moved with the seasons and the herds.

On the way to the Coppermine, they would undoubtedly meet other bands that might take advantage of a lone European, but Matonabbee's status would ensure the foreigner's safety. At the end of their journey, however, they would cross into the territory of the Inuit, who were enemies to the Dene. He knew how his warriors would likely react to the Inuit, and having the Englishman along would complicate things. But he'd promised the governor to guide Hearne to his destination and back.

They would be gone a long time, probably a year or more, so they had to rely on the land for their food. Even with dogs pulling sleds, they could never carry enough. So they traveled in the Dene fashion, following the deer, staying near the edge of the woods.

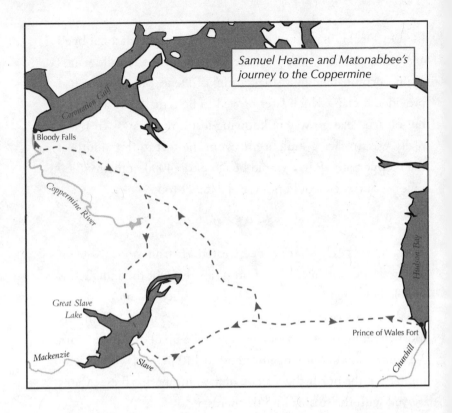

Samuel Hearne and Matonabbee's journey to the Coppermine

When there was plenty of meat, they gorged. One time, Matonabbee ate so much that he had to be towed on a sled. He didn't regret it, though. They never knew when they'd find their next meal. When there was no game, days would pass when only melted snow and tobacco touched their lips. Sometimes, they ate last season's cranberries, dried on bushes, even though the fruit made their stomachs cramp. They even cut off a bit of leather from their clothing to chew on. Instead of complaining, they joked about it.

They walked from the first sign of pale winter dawn light until darkness fell, only a few hours later. On cold days when the snow was dry, walking was easy. If it became too warm, wet snow hung off their snowshoes in heavy clumps. To the north, they could see the Barren Lands: rocky and treeless, with a spare beauty to them.

Although the wilderness was vast and, to Hearne's eye, empty, the travelers were not exactly alone. In fact, this supposedly "barren" land was home to thousands of people. Over the months, they met up with other bands, usually Dene, who might join them for a feast or walk with them a few days.

One group, the Yellowknife Dene, had never seen a European before, and examined Hearne as if he were a newly discovered animal. He was an acceptable human being, they concluded, except for the color of his hair, eyes, and skin. His eyes were too pale, and his skin looked like meat that had been left in water until all the blood had soaked out. Even so, they were very friendly, and Hearne regretted having so little to offer as a gift.

Any encounter with another group was an occasion to exchange news and gifts, and barter for supplies. Assuming Hearne was a fur trader (the only kind of white man most knew), people would ask him for tobacco or gunpowder. Often Matonabbee responded by giving from his own supplies.

These gatherings were also opportunities to buy or win another man's wife by challenging him to a wrestling match. A Dene man's importance was reflected by his number of wives. Hearne observed with mixed emotions, never thinking that this custom might bring his journey to an end. But it nearly did.

In one match, Matonabbee won a pretty young wife from a younger man. Then he bought another wife, a skilled woman, from a giant warrior. One night in May, the young wife ran away to rejoin her former husband. Matonabbee, the most important man of his nation, was shamed. How could a woman choose a weak young man over himself? The next day, the giant warrior announced that he wanted *his* wife back. Matonabbee knew that even he was no match for this man. So he was forced to bargain to keep her, and gave the other man a large quantity of ammunition, tools, iron, and a copper kettle.

Feeling he had lost his honor, Matonabbee refused to continue. He would find Hearne a guide to escort him back to the fort.

Hearne knew they'd come farther west already than on his previous journeys and Matonabbee was the best guide he could hope to have. He tried desperately to persuade his guide to proceed, emphasizing that the governor and his successors would hold the Dene man in high regard. Finally, Matonabbee agreed.

They were heading north of what is now Great Slave Lake in the Northwest Territories. To Hearne's dismay, the warriors in their group were planning a raid on the Inuit known to camp around the Coppermine River. At first, Hearne tried to persuade them to make peace. But he quickly realized that the feud between the two nations had lasted for as long as anyone could remember. Not wanting to offend his guides, he declared that, while the Inuit were not his enemy, he would do all he could to protect his companions.

Leaving most of the party to wait for their return, Hearne, Matonabbee, and a large group of warriors continued north hastily. For this excursion, it made sense to leave women and children behind. They walked for 12 hours or longer each day. By now, they were well north of the Arctic Circle and it was summer—season of the midnight sun—when the sun almost never set.

On July 2, 1771, a surprise summer snowstorm slowed them down. Only days later, they trudged along under a hot sun. When they reached the Stony Mountains, they scrambled over slippery rubble, at times forced to crawl on their hands and knees. The volatile weather turned from sleet to snow to sunshine. They were soaked to the skin for days at a time. When it got too bad, they sheltered in dank caves; during one fierce snowstorm, they feared they'd be buried alive in their cave. When the weather finally broke, the mosquitoes were so thick, the men could hardly sleep.

Despite these difficulties, on July 14 they reached Hearne's destination—the Coppermine River. He gazed across it in dismay. The narrow, shallow river was full of rocks and punctuated with small waterfalls. It was nothing like the mighty waterway he'd heard about. A few spindly trees were scattered here and there, but he couldn't imagine how a fort could be established in such a place.

He spent the next two days surveying the river. Meanwhile, two scouts were sent ahead to look for bands of Inuit. One more time, he voiced his doubts about the planned raid, but Matonabbee just shook his head. "Perhaps the scouts will find no enemies," he replied, frustrated by Hearne's lack of comprehension.

Early on the third day, the scouts returned with news that five Inuit tents had been spotted less than a day's journey downstream. All thoughts of the Englishman's survey work were forgotten. The war party crossed the river.

As they neared the circle of tents, they sank low to the ground, watching the unsuspecting group finish the day's tasks and prepare for sleep. While they waited, the warriors went about their final preparations for battle—tying back or cutting their hair, painting their faces red and black and, ignoring the hungry mosquitoes, stripping down to a minimal amount of clothing.

They urged Hearne to stay behind, but he feared that an

escaping Inuit would stumble on him and assume that he too was the enemy. So he tied back his hair and peeled off his cap and stockings, saying that he would follow the warriors into battle, but would hurt no one himself.

Finally, at about one in the morning, the warriors sprang from their ambush. They were nearly upon the silent tents before those sleeping inside were aware. About 20 Inuit burst out and tried to flee. None survived. Hearne was horrified. In a daze, he stumbled toward the rapids nearby and named them Bloody Falls, to commemorate what he had witnessed.

Afterward, the warriors noticed more tents on the east side of the river. It was too wide to cross, so the Dene began shooting at the Inuit on the other bank. The Inuit had never seen guns before, and watched with curiosity, examining the flattened lead bullets. When one man was struck in the leg, they finally understood they were in danger and retreated to their canoes, paddling out of range.

The warriors also jumped into canoes, and paddled across the Coppermine to plunder the tents. A few Inuit had returned to gather their belongings, but most had fled to safety. One man who lingered too long was not so lucky. As the rest of the Inuit watched helplessly from their canoes, the Dene killed the Inuit man, then ransacked the camp, throwing tents, tent poles, and stores of food into the river.

Their mission completed, the warriors reverted to their normal behavior as if nothing had happened, and cooked a meal of fresh salmon.

Historians since have wondered if the attack was an act of revenge, or spiritually motivated. To the Dene, the spirit world was just as real as the physical one, and actions that happened in one realm affected the other. They believed the spirit world required a number of deaths each year, so by killing others they appeased the spirits and protected their own lives.

To Hearne, however, their motives were incomprehensible and he was tempted to leave the warriors—but he would certainly die in the wilderness alone.

In the end he chose to survive, so sat down at the fire and ate with the others.

"Now we will finish your survey," Matonabbee said. The results were discouraging. The Company's idea of transporting goods by boat was impossible. Even in summer, thick ice rimmed the shore. No boat could cut through it.

As was the custom, he wrote his name and the date, July 17, 1771, on a shield and secured it with rocks near the mouth of the river. In this way, he "claimed" the land for the Hudson's Bay Company. All he had left to do was find the copper mine he'd heard so much about.

Following a Yellowknife man who knew the area, they started toward the mine, but exhaustion forced them to lie down for the first time in three days. After a few hours' sleep, one of the warriors killed an old muskox. It was raining hard enough that a fire was impossible, so they ate it raw.

Arriving at the mine site, the whole party searched the area, but found only one sizable lump of copper. Obviously, the site had been a good source of copper at one time, but had been picked clean by generations of native miners. Hearne couldn't believe that he'd traveled so far and faced so many challenges just to discover that the Company's dream was unfounded. All hopes for his own advancement and fame evaporated. Hearne felt utterly defeated.

With their obligations fulfilled, Matonabbee and the warriors were anxious to rejoin the rest of the party. They headed south as fast as they could, stopping only when necessary. Their pace was relentless, and Hearne's lower legs and feet swelled so much that he could barely walk.

"I left the print of my feet in blood almost at every step I took," he later wrote.

IT WOULD TAKE HEARNE and Matonabbee nearly a year to return to Prince of Wales Fort. On June 30, 1772, an exhausted, hungry, disappointed Hearne approached the gates. He and Matonabbee had been traveling for 18 months and 23 days. In all his attempts combined, he'd walked between 5500 and 8000 kilometers (3500 to 5000 miles).

He'd sent a letter ahead to the governor, saying that he would arrive soon, but was still surprised to see crowds of people waiting. A cannon fired and cheers hailed him as he approached. Despite his protests, several young men hoisted him onto their shoulders and carried him into the fort to a hero's welcome.

In Hearne's mind, the arduous northern crossing had been a failure, but he had returned with valuable information, including a detailed map of the region. Although not completely accurate, it was a remarkable feat considering the conditions he'd endured and his inadequate instruments. His long journey also dispelled several rumors. By the time Hearne returned, the Hudson's Bay Company had already squandered large sums of money in their search for the fabled copper mine. Hearne's report saved them from wasting more money and effort. He also settled the question of whether there was a "northwest passage"—an inland waterway from Hudson Bay to the northern ocean—that would enable trade between Europe, the New World, and Asia. Hearne reported that the only passage remained the ice-packed ocean.

He later wrote a book about his journey, published three years after his death. It instructed Europeans on the best way to explore the north—to travel as the local people did. His observations of the people, animals, plants, and terrain still tell historians a lot about life back then.

Apart from a shield wedged between rocks and a trail of bloody footprints, Hearne did leave a mark on the world. After a distinguished career that included serving as governor of Prince of Wales Fort, he retired to England. For the rest of his life, he felt compelled to tell people about the terrible event he'd participated in at Bloody Falls. His story reached the poet Samuel Taylor Coleridge, who created a haunted traveler in his famous epic poem, *The Rime of the Ancient Mariner.*

Crossing a War Zone

Western Germany, 1945

SEIGFRIED HOFFMANN HAD JUST RETURNED to the camp barracks from his day's work on the Weissmann farm when he and the other boys were told to assemble in the sitting room. Two very important visitors were there to meet them. Immediately, he knew something was wrong, or at least, more wrong than usual.

From their uniforms, he could tell the two visitors were officers in the SS, the elite unit of the Nazi Party, made up of men who pledged unconditional loyalty to Germany's leader, the *Führer* Adolf Hitler.

The officers stood stiffly before the boys, their faces stern. The situation of the war was very serious, they said. It was up to all Germans to fight for their country. Then they launched into a long pro-Nazi speech. Siegfried had heard so many and hated to listen—lies and propaganda, that's all it was. *We are a proud and strong people. We must be loyal to our community and the Fatherland. Our honor is our faithfulness.*

Although Seigfried and the other boys were at "camp" in Steisslingen, it was a Hitler Youth Camp. German youth groups had started in the 1890s as informal gatherings of boys who wanted to hike, sleep under the stars, and sing German folk songs. But by the late 1930s, they'd become instruments for the government to prepare youth for the military. Now the law said that every German child over 10 years old had to enroll in a Hitler Youth Camp and obey all orders. By late in World War II, these orders were given by belligerent, self-appointed teenage leaders—barely older than Seigfried himself. All the men had been recruited to fight on the front lines.

The officers described the final upcoming victory. But this was early April 1945; Germany was losing the war and the American army was only about 160 km (100 miles) away and coming closer every day. Although they were still boys, Seigfried and the others knew this, but Hitler's soldiers refused to admit defeat.

When he had first risen to power in the 1930s, Hitler had promised to lead Germany to a better future. He would rebuild the nation, which had been devastated by World War I and the following Depression. Under Hitler's leadership, people had jobs, money, and a major highway. But one of the Nazi Party's aims was to create a new empire made up of all ethnic German areas across Europe. It would be ruled by a race of pure Germans: tall, strong, obedient, blond, and blue-eyed. When Hitler invaded Poland in September 1939, Britain and France declared war on Germany.

For the first three years, Germany was winning. At their strongest, the Axis powers (including Germany, Italy, and Japan) controlled most of Europe as well as part of northern Africa. But since 1942, they'd been losing ground.

During that time, millions of Jews, as well as homosexuals, gypsies, and other people the Nazis targeted, were being exterminated in concentration camps. It's hard to know if Seigfried was aware of the concentration camps; however, he was opposed to Hitler and the Nazis.

As a teenager, Seigfried only knew that he wanted the war to end. And that night, the officers' false words made him feel sick to his stomach. Then it got worse: the German army needed to draft 12 boys for the honor of fighting side by side with experienced soldiers—they made it sound like this was a *good* thing.

The boys were ordered to form a single line. The officers were looking for the tallest, strongest, and healthiest among them. Seigfried tried to shrink into himself, but it was no use. At barely 15 years old, he was nearly two meters in height (over six feet), with the wide shoulders of a full-grown man, blue eyes, and ash-blond hair. They pulled him forward.

"You are now part of the German army," one officer told the chosen boys. "We will pick you up in the next two days." With a curt salute to the camp leader, they left, their heels striking loudly against the wooden floor.

The room was completely silent; Seigfried was numb with fear. They were being sent to their deaths.

THAT EVENING, he slipped out of the barracks and walked to the Weissmanns' farm. As a contribution to the war effort, every boy had to work on a local farm. Seigfried had been assigned to the Weissmanns, an older couple with no children. He'd worked hard, planting, tilling, and harvesting. But he liked the work and in turn, the Weissmanns treated him like a son.

Now, sitting at their kitchen table, he told them what had happened. Mr. Weissmann sat down and lit his pipe. For a long time he said nothing, then he put his hand on Seigfried's shoulder and said, "Go back to the barracks. Go to bed and pretend you are sleeping. When all the others are asleep and you feel it's safe enough, come back here with only what is dearest and most important to you."

So that's what Seigfried did.

After he'd returned to the farm, he fell into a deep sleep until Mr. Weissmann shook him awake. It was still dark outside.

"Dress in these clothes," he said, pointing to a pile at the foot of the bed. They were Mr. Weissmann's clothes, altered to fit. The couple had obviously been awake all night, preparing clothes and packing a knapsack with extra clothes, food, and other essentials.

"You must leave immediately," Mr. Weissmann said. "It's no longer safe for you here." All three were crying.

It felt as awful as when he'd had to say goodbye to his mother, stepfather, and older sister Sigrid, just over a year ago. Both he and Sigrid had been sent from their home in Strasbourg, near the French-German border, to the south, farther from the front lines. Sigrid was in a girls' camp in nearby Markdorf, so Seigfried decided to go see her.

THE ONLY WAY TO GET PAST the barracks and the village without being seen was to walk north through the farmyards encircling Steisslingen. It seemed as if every dog in the area barked out the news of his passing. Blinded by the darkness, he stumbled over pails, farm machinery, fences, and manure piles. Eventually, he made it to the road outside town.

Steisslingen is in southwest Germany, near the north shore of Lake Boden. On the other side of the lake lay the neutral country of Switzerland. From the barracks, he used to see lights shining from Swiss towns and cities, and wondered what it felt like to be so free that everyone could leave lights shining all evening. For years Germany had lived in darkness, every window blacked out to protect them from bombing raids.

When he arrived at the farm where Sigrid worked, the sun was shining. She was washing the breakfast dishes and came out to give him a hug. After getting him some breakfast, they caught up on each other's news.

Over the next two days, he helped around the farm and discussed with Sigrid what to do. Most of all, they wanted to be with their parents in Strasbourg. When their mother had married Herr Hoffmann, they'd moved from their hometown of Münster in the northwest to their stepfather's home. Strasbourg was in the Alsace region, a small pocket of land that the French and Germans had fought over for hundreds of years. Now it was in France, though effectively run by Germany.

Seigfried and Sigrid had heard that all Germans there had been imprisoned by the French just before the American army arrived. Even so, they didn't believe this might have happened to their parents, and decided to go to Strasbourg.

Seigfried couldn't help but feel excited. They were embarking on a real-life *adventure*. He didn't know then that he'd end up covering over 850 kilometers (525 miles)—farther than the full length of the country—almost entirely on foot.

War had devastated Germany. Most radio networks were out of commission and few trains for civilians were still in operation. Seigfried and Sigrid had heard that some trains were still running between Strasbourg and Ludwigshafen, a small town 210 kilometers (130 miles) to the north. Although Strasbourg was closer, they had to avoid the Allied troops advancing from the west, so they began to walk north.

Seigfried hoped the Allies could end the chaos, even though they were the enemy. Once the war was over, he might have a chance of a normal life again—if he survived, that is.

As he and Sigrid trudged on, their every thought and action was overshadowed by fear. The Allies were close, though it was impossible to know just how close. For the next few days, they pushed aside thoughts of danger by talking, arguing, or laughing together. Usually, he teased his older sister or found her irritating, but a year's separation and the very real possibility of losing her changed things. She wasn't so bad, after all.

By the time they reached Ludwigshafen, they were exhausted.

They were told their train would leave at nine the next morning. The station's waiting room was already crowded with soldiers and civilians, and the stench of sweat, grime, and desperation permeated the airless room. Some people were sleeping despite the racket, some crying, others yelling loudly that their belongings were being stolen.

Not wanting to eat in front of others—who might have no food themselves—they sneaked outside and gulped down some of their scanty provisions. As they walked back into the station, a soldier entered. Seeing the two children on their own, he took them under his wing.

Throughout the night, Mr. Kowalsky—his civilian name, he explained—told them stories of fighting on the front line. In turn, they told him their plans to meet their parents in Strasbourg. He urged them to stay put, but gave up once he saw their determination.

"COME ON, YOU TWO WARRIORS, WAKE UP." Mr. Kowalsky shook Seigfried's shoulder and grinned, showing teeth that hadn't seen a toothbrush for a long time. "Listen, children," he said, "if you have to go to Strasbourg, come outside now." It was just after six in the morning and people had started to wake.

Inhaling the fresh air greedily, they followed him toward the tracks. "When the train arrives," he said, "it will already be half full. As you can see," he jerked his head toward the crowded waiting room, "there are more people in there than will fit on the train. Now listen, this is war. People get killed during a war. People will get killed here this morning, trying to get on that train. Don't think about the babies or old people. You must think of yourselves. That is, if you want to stay alive. Remember, no one will help you. Wait here."

Kowalsky walked a ways down the tracks to a water tower, then returned. "Come," he said. As he walked back toward the tower, they could hear him counting his steps until he stopped abruptly. "Here is where you should be when the train arrives."

Then he led them halfway back to the water tower. "Stand here and pretend to be waiting. Most people coming out of the waiting room will stand with us. You'll see. It's human nature to follow the leader."

Especially for Germans, thought Seigfried.

Sure enough, soon a crowd gathered around them.

"I will have to leave you to take an army car up front," Kowalsky continued in a low voice. "When I say go, run back to your spot, but stand back. Make sure there is room for three or four rows of people between you and the tracks. Those behind will push, so the people in front will be forced onto the tracks and under the train. Remember, don't stumble or you'll be trampled to death."

This sounded so unbelievable, Seigfried was sure he must be exaggerating or joking, but his expression was serious. As he spoke, more and more people poured out of the waiting room. After giving this advice, he went to stand with the other soldiers.

When Mr. Kowalsky heard the train approaching, he shouted, "GO!" They ran as fast as they could while pandemonium erupted. Everyone was screaming, pushing, and scrambling to board the train. The crowd was too crazed to care who got hurt.

By carefully following their friend's instructions, they squeezed onto a civilian car and found a spot near a window, though the bombing had blown all the glass out long before. With a lurch, the train pulled out. The fresh air coming in the window was welcome. Soon enough, they would be even more grateful for that open window.

Between two of its regular stops, the train lurched to a stand-still. Ahead the rails lay broken, destroyed by bombs. On the other side of the gap in the track, another train waited, headed in the same direction. Within seconds Seigfried and Sigrid were out of the window and running toward the new train. Not only did they make it, they even got a seat.

Meanwhile, the first train erupted in panic. Desperate to get out, many leaped out of windows, only to be crushed by others jumping on top, or heavy baggage being tossed out. Many people died there. Those struggling to get onto the new train kicked and elbowed, cursing and pulling hair in a frantic battle to survive.

Packed tightly into his spot on the railway car, Seigfried couldn't move. In all the excitement, he'd ignored the need to pee. He couldn't hold it any longer. The relief was so great, he didn't even mind the cold pants clinging to his legs or the puddle at his feet.

"How could you?" Sigrid hissed at him in disgust.

Just wait, he thought. *It will happen to you some time.*

THE TRAIN CONTINUED SOUTHWEST until it came to its final stop at a little station called Neuheim, an hour and a half's walk from Strasbourg. Seigfried and Sigrid were only too happy to get away from the crush of people.

The small town of Kehl lay on the German side of the border, with Strasbourg on the other side in France. Between the two cities ran the Rhine River. Once off the train, they headed for Kehl. They avoided the roads, following Kowalsky's warning that not only would fighter-bombers spot them on the open road and shoot them down, but stronger travelers would steal everything they had. Crossing meadows and little creeks, they walked through tall grass and thistles. Worse, though, were the hundreds of craters from fallen bombs and grenades. The fighting in that area had obviously been very recent, as the Allied troops moved east across Germany. Burned-out army equipment lay scattered around. Hastily dug graves littered the ground, some so shallow that a boot or hand or face poked out. Their earlier eagerness for adventure was dampened by this grim reality.

With the Rhine River bridge in sight, they didn't notice the German officers until they were stopped by the barrels of two guns.

"Where have you come from?" the younger officer snapped, pushing the gun closer. "How did you get here without permission? Where are you going?"

Terrified, they shakily told the soldiers their plans. The younger one then led them behind a burned-out tank. From there, they had a clear view of the full length of the bridge. At least 20 people were on it. Then they noticed the twisted, awkward positions of their bodies—dead.

The soldier pointed again. Amidst the dead bodies, they noticed a faint, almost imperceptible, rustle. Three people crouched low, each dragging a dead body as protection from the bullets. Crawling backward, they were inching toward the German side of the border.

"They have no chance," the officer was saying when, *wham*, a grenade blew the three right through the deck of the bridge.

"The Germans on the other side have been put into prison camps," the other officer explained. Strasbourg had been reclaimed by the French and the Allies. "Even if by chance you make it across, you will not find your parents. Go back to the Fatherland."

Terrified and disappointed, they turned back. Where were their parents, and were they still alive? And what could they do now?

There was no way Seigfried could return to the Hitler Youth Camp in Steisslingen. The safest place for him would be their

Uncle Jacob's in Heidelberg, a city near Ludwigshafen. As for Sigrid, she no longer felt safe, a 16-year-old girl with only her younger brother for protection. There were half-crazed soldiers everywhere. She'd return to Markdorf. The difficult decision made, they headed northeast—back to the train station.

What they didn't know was that Hitler's empire was rapidly disintegrating. Far away under the streets of Berlin, Adolf Hitler and his senior staff had retreated to his underground headquarters, the *Führerbunker*. On April 30, Hitler and his new bride Eva Braun committed suicide, followed the next day by the propaganda minister, Joseph Goebbels, and his wife and six children. The bodies were all burned.

Meanwhile, in the southwest, Seigfried and Sigrid hitched a ride partway to Ludwigshafen, completely unaware of the larger dramas unfolding.

The couple who picked them up were "organizing" in preparation for life after the war. "Organizing" was a wartime expression that meant stealing. The couple was organizing enough goods to stock their hardware store, now empty and destroyed by bombs. They were already looking toward the future. After a short ride, they dropped off Seigfried and Sigrid.

By this time their food had run out. As they walked, they "organized" a chicken, potatoes, and milk from a cow.

In two days, they reached Ludwigshafen, which had been recently bombed. At the railway station, miraculously, a train heading south toward Markdorf was waiting and only half full.

One woman even held out a hand to help Sigrid board. Suddenly the train was off, before brother and sister had the chance to say goodbye. Seigfried stood and watched the train disappear, wondering if he'd ever see her again.

THE TRAIN STATION WAS FULL of wounded soldiers and people carrying bags and boxes bound with string. Drizzling rain came through the broken windows, soaking him.

As he walked toward the exit, he passed several doors. One opened to a first aid room. He picked up some bandages and supplies that might later be useful for trading. Poking his head into the next room, he saw a bed, complete with pillow, sheets, and blanket. No one was nearby, so he closed the door behind him. He hung his clothes up to dry, crawled under the covers, and closed his eyes.

As he lay there, a loneliness overcame him that was so powerful it felt like it was crushing him. Eventually his fatigue allowed him to escape into a long sleep.

He left the station before sunrise. Outside, the air was filled with concrete dust and the acrid smell of smoke from burning timber and dead bodies. Every building was destroyed, or so damaged it would need to be torn down. People sorted purposefully through the rubble for intact bricks, which were then cleaned of old mortar and neatly stacked in rows. Others pushed refuse into big piles. Their work suggested a new beginning, though Seigfried couldn't imagine what a new life might look like.

Once out of the town, he struggled over fences, through fields and creeks. Without knowing if his Uncle Jacob was still alive, he headed for Heidelberg, about 110 kilometers (70 miles) to the east. He had no guide other than the sun, but as long as he didn't get lost, it should take him less than a week to walk there.

Seigfried set himself a point on the horizon and walked toward it, climbing over hills and down valleys. He'd seen enough of war to develop an acute sense of when German or American troops were near, and was always calculating where the fighting might be.

As he traveled, he used skills he'd learned in the Hitler Youth: making fire pits and shelters, cutting boughs to sleep on. One afternoon he caught a fish using only a safety pin, string, and worm. Pride filled him as he watched the fish sizzling over his fire. If only he'd caught more—he could easily eat ten.

After days of walking, he realized he was off course and would need to walk due west to reach Heidelberg. This meant he would have to pass through the densely populated war zone. If he heard soldiers speaking German, he was no longer worried. One soldier actually drew him a map of the way to Heidelberg.

It was now May 1945 and the Germans had declared their unconditional surrender to the Allies. The process of ending a war was a long one, however. German soldiers who had been discharged were retreating, though many didn't know what they were retreating to. Everyone he met seemed as bewildered as Seigfried himself.

When he finally reached his uncle and aunt's house, no one answered his knock. He crossed the city to his cousin Anni's house, and they talked over coffee. Food and fuel for heat were low, she said, confessing that she didn't know how she would feed her 18-month-old child, Horst. Her father, Seigfried's Uncle Jacob, had been taken prisoner and she hadn't heard from her husband in weeks.

Her apartment was large and modern. Its expensive carpets and furniture and beautiful china contrasted starkly to their meager rations. Not knowing where else to go, Seigfried stayed with Anni.

At first, Seigfried hoped his parents would also come to Heidelberg, because it was near Strasbourg. After a few weeks, he gave up hope. Then he remembered what his mother had once said: if and when the war ever ended and if they couldn't find each other, they would meet on the steps of the cathedral in Münster. The war was over now, so he said goodbye to Anni and Horst and set off on foot once again.

Almost half of Germany lay between him and Münster in the northwest. By now he was a seasoned survivor, but what he saw was so shocking it would haunt him for the rest of his life. The route he had to take cut through what had only recently been the front line. The wreckage of war lay all around. He stumbled past dead bodies, destroyed cities, and burned-out trucks and tanks.

One evening after a couple of weeks, he heard the voices of German soldiers in a field. He hurried out of the woods toward their camp. But it was dusk and hard to see properly, and everyone was trigger-happy. Suddenly he heard shots, and bullets whistled past. Not thinking, he ran back toward the woods. After a few steps, a burning sensation sliced through his leg, but he kept running into the safety of the trees.

Once hidden, he stopped and saw that a bullet had torn clean through his knee. Blood dripped down his leg. Using the bandages in his pack, he bound his knee as best he could, despite the stabbing pain.

The following day, he was able to limp to the closest village for help. After resting a couple of days, he continued more slowly. When at last he walked into Münster, relief alternated with sadness as he surveyed the bombed streets of his hometown. Even the great St. Paul's cathedral was partially ruined, but he was happy to see it.

He sat down on the front steps, his journey over. The pain in his knee had subsided to a dull ache. When he asked passersby if they had seen his parents, they shook their heads. Everyone was busy with their own problems: finding loved ones, rebuilding what they'd lost.

Night fell. Seigfried was used to sleeping almost anywhere, but it still felt strange to spend the night on the street. He was most afraid of having his few belongings stolen, so slept lightly.

For weeks, Seigfried sat on the cathedral steps and waited. What if he never saw his family again? He tried not to think about that.

One day he spotted two familiar-looking figures far down the street. It took him only a moment to react. He jumped up—his mother and Sigrid! They walked toward him as if out of a dream. He ran over and threw his arms around them. They held each other in a fierce, tearful, three-way embrace.

ALTHOUGH HE NEVER TALKED about the mass murders in the concentration camps, known as the Holocaust, Seigfried would surely have known about them after the war. Following Germany's surrender, the Allies began restructuring the country. In the British- and American-run areas, documentaries about the camps were shown to schoolchildren. Still, few could bring themselves to talk about it openly. Like most people everywhere, Seigfried loved his country and its people, making it all the harder to accept what they had done.

Seigfried stayed in Germany for 10 years before immigrating to Canada in the mid-1950s. Over the next decades, he built a life for himself as a foreman in a mine, married, and had two daughters.

Eventually, Seigfried wrote a series of letters to his teenage daughters. In them, he described the terrible realities of the war and the last days of his childhood. In 1987, he died at 57 years old.

Cold War Swim

Bering Strait, Alaska to USSR, August 7, 1987

IN A SWIMSUIT, CAP, AND GOGGLES, 30-year-old Lynne Cox perched on the boat's edge. She slid into the water feet first. Icy cold, it stole the breath out of her lungs. Bouncing to the surface, she lunged through the water to shore, then scrambled over the sharp rocks. But her swim wasn't over yet—she'd only arrived at the *starting* line.

As she stood in the shallow water off the shore of Little Diomede Island in northern Alaska, Lynne surveyed the people who would accompany her on this historic crossing to Big Diomede Island. They were all there to ensure she made it across this stretch of the Bering Strait alive. The strait, separating the westernmost point of North America and the easternmost point of Asia, was not only a physical division, but a political one. Although only 4.35 kilometers (2.7 miles) of ocean lay between the two islands, their inhabitants hadn't seen each other in 48 years. The real barrier was the international border that ran between them. In 1939, the US–USSR border had been closed due to the Second World War. Ever since 1945, growing tensions between the two superpowers—known as the Cold War—meant that nuclear attack was always a looming threat.

Lynne's hope was that her swim would, in some small way, encourage cooperation between the two countries. No one had ever made such a crossing; Lynne was aiming to be the first.

Journalists and camera crew filled two walrus-skinned boats, or *umiaks*. Her medical support crew perched in an inflatable Zodiac with their monitoring and emergency first-aid equipment. The guides, Pat Omiak and David Soolook, lived in Little Diomede village. More villagers filled five other *umiaks*. They all looked at Lynne expectantly. Despite the cold, she was beaming. For the past 11 years, she'd been hoping, dreaming, and planning for this day. With a splash, she dove in.

She was swimming to the Soviet Union.

"PLEASE DON'T TELL ME how cold the water is," Lynne had told the crew before they left. On this swim she could freeze to death, literally. Afterward, she found out the water was a chilly 42° Fahrenheit (5.5° Celsius). At 32° F (0° C), fresh water freezes.

Three doctors—Dr. Keatinge, Dr. Nyboer Jr., and Dr. Nyboer Sr.—were there to study Lynne. They hoped to find out more about how humans regulate their body temperature. Before the swim, Dr. Keatinge had given Lynne a silver capsule the size of a horse pill, called a thermopill, to swallow. It would measure her core temperature. For the duration of the swim, it would float inside her, monitoring how well, or poorly, her body was coping with the extreme conditions. The doctor worried that it would be difficult to swallow, but Lynne was more concerned about how to get it *out* afterward.

If her body temperature dropped by more than 4°F (2.5°C), hypothermia would set in—her body would be too cold to reheat itself and she would eventually lose control of her limbs, then slip into unconsciousness. The doctors would pull her from the water. In water this cold, that could take only half an hour. After an hour or so in such frigid water, most people would die—and this swim was expected to take about two hours. But Lynne was not most people.

A mixture of good genes and dedicated training enabled Lynne to perform truly amazing athletic feats. Most athletes don't want fat, but Lynne cultivated hers. Her layer of body fat was spread unusually evenly, right down her limbs. Typically, men's fat gathers around their stomachs and women's fat settles on their hips and thighs. Lynne compared herself to a whale or a seal, animals whose even layers of fat keep them warm. "Their blubber is very dense," she added, "whereas mine is more like a cotton sweater." Instead of seeing fat as embarrassing, she recognized early on the great advantage it gave her in her sport.

Of course, under the fat were powerful muscles and a strong heart and lungs. When her muscles worked hard, they generated heat. In order to endure a long swim, Lynne needed to create more heat than the cold water took away. Any cold-weather athlete has to generate sufficient heat: when a jogger runs on a cold day, he feels warm because his body is warmer than the air.

Lynne also had a rare neutral buoyancy: she didn't sink or float, because her body was the same density as water. Thanks to this, all her energy went into moving forward, rather than being wasted on either keeping afloat or pulling downward through the water.

Yet getting to this point hadn't been easy. She'd started planning 11 years earlier and even then, permission from the Soviets only came through the day before the swim. For years, she'd written letters, made phone calls and appointments with officials to gain permission and support. At one point she was even followed by the

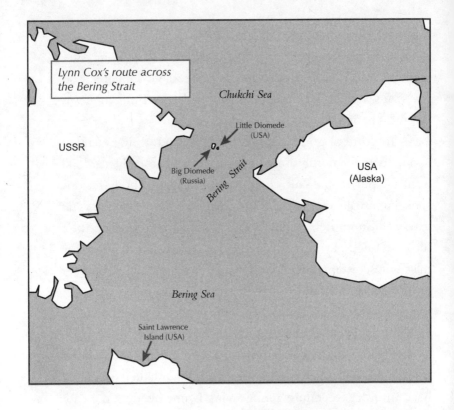

Lynn Cox's route across the Bering Strait

Chukchi Sea

Little Diomede
(USA)

USSR

Big Diomede
(Russia)

Bering Strait

USA
(Alaska)

Bering Sea

Saint Lawrence
Island (USA)

American FBI and Soviet KGB. Both countries suspected she was a spy! But she was simply determined to complete this swim.

Lynne sometimes felt as if she'd spent her entire life preparing for this day. In her family, all four children swam on a team in Long Beach, California. When she was nine, a team practice in an outdoor pool had almost been cancelled because of a hailstorm. Lynne not only finished the workout but discovered she loved slicing through the soupy, half-frozen water. Her parents encouraged her to try open-water swimming, and by the time she was 14, she was strong enough to cross from Catalina Island to the California mainland, a 12½-hour swim. To train, she acclimatized herself to the cold by sleeping without blankets and with the window open, wearing light clothing even during winter.

At 15, she broke the men's and women's record for crossing the English Channel. When another American broke her record three weeks later, she returned to England the following year and completed the famous crossing again. She shaved eight minutes off the new record.

She never swam with anything other than a swimsuit, goggles, and a bathing cap: no wetsuit, no protective grease. "I feel the cold just like anyone else," she once said. She just didn't dwell on it. "If you focus on the cold, then you're focusing on something that's not helping you get to where you need to get."

LYNNE LOOKED DOWN at her hands pulling through the gray-blue water. Her fingers were pressed together firmly, forming strong paddles. If she couldn't control her fingers, she'd know hypothermia was setting in, but so far all was good.

At that moment, she felt strong and powerful and quickly passed the two escort *umiaks*. The water was unusually calm.

The only problem was the fog. For weeks she and her crew had waited for good weather conditions in Little Diomede village. By the time she reached the village, news of her swim was stirring up excitement. Television and radio crews were on standby for the big event. All they had needed was permission from the Soviets to cross the maritime border, which lay at about the halfway point of her swim. With the border open for this one day, the Soviets were expecting them at noon. They couldn't wait for better weather; they might never get permission again.

Fifteen minutes into her swim, fog enveloped them in a thick gray blanket. Each time she turned her head for a breath, the escort boats were harder and harder to make out in the gloom. Soon they disappeared altogether.

All she could see was cold gray sea. The escort boats were supposed to stay right beside her and guide her, but they had drifted too far away. She couldn't afford to go off course. Every minute in this freezing water brought her closer to the limit of endurance. Behind her, she could just make out the doctors in their Zodiac. When she yelled, they didn't answer, too busy with their medical equipment.

"Are we going straight?" she called out. "Go straight ahead!" Dr. Keatinge replied as her guides moved their *umiaks* closer. Reassured, she plunged forward.

Soon after, the doctors pulled close and waved. "We need to take your temperature." Lynne paddled up to the Zodiac and rolled onto her back.

Because of her phenomenal ability to withstand the cold, Lynne had acted as a test subject in several studies. But the doctors' new equipment was fussy and it took a long time for them to get a reading from the thermopill. As they were fiddling with their equipment, Lynne was losing valuable heat. After what felt like an eternity, they got a reading and she swam away.

They were about halfway by then, but with the fog so thick it was hard to tell. With each breath, Lynne looked for the Soviet boat. Soviet officials had promised to send a boat to meet her party as they crossed the border. But she saw nothing.

Worse, the current was steadily pushing them north. Big Diomede Island, their destination, was not actually that big— barely a speck on the map. If they missed it, they could be swept out into the cold, open Chukchi Sea. Then they'd be in trouble.

Abruptly, both escort boats veered sharply to the left. *What are they doing?* Lynne wondered as she followed them.

After a while, heavy drizzle started to fall. Dr. Keatinge and Dr. Nyboer asked her to stop so that they could get another temperature reading. After several futile attempts, Lynne impatiently rolled over and sprinted away. She was frightened and above all, cold. The guide boats wove left, then right. Pushing aside her fear, Lynne concentrated on moving her arms as quickly as possible.

She didn't know that her guides were lost. Although both were experienced walrus hunters, they did not know the waters this far out from their home on Little Diomede. Forbidden from hunting in Soviet territory, they only knew the area on the American side.

Luckily, no one guessed how lost they really were, or how far north they'd drifted. Unaware of the danger, Lynne kept swimming, wondering if the Soviets had changed their minds at the last minute.

The day before, when she'd heard that the Soviets would allow her to land, she couldn't believe it. Officials from all over the USSR were traveling to Big Diomede to meet her. They'd even offered to provide whatever she needed for the end of the swim. She asked for blankets, a hot water bottle, hot drinks, and a traditional Russian headscarf, a *babushka*. The brightly colored fabric, she thought, would add a nice symbolic touch.

She was on the verge of panic when she heard a low hum through the water. It faded, then came back. Soon the crew heard it too. It had to be the Soviet boat searching for them. The drone grew louder, then the pitch changed…it was moving away. Everyone shouted as loud as they could until the sound grew stronger again, to their great relief.

The dark gray hull of the Soviet boat was a beautiful sight to Lynne, and her goggles fogged up with happy tears. She hadn't really believed the Soviets would arrive. But her crew had managed to get back on course and the Soviets had found them in the fog.

She called out to the Soviets to move closer and was surprised to hear a man answer back in perfect English. "My name is Vladimir McMillan," he called from the deck of the boat high above the water. The Soviet crew, at first somber-faced, slowly broke into smiles.

With the excitement, Lynne's stroke rate had dropped to a dangerously slow speed. She wasn't generating enough heat to keep warm. Her first priority had to be speed, so she put her head down and paddled hard.

Her whole face felt as if it had been frozen by the dentist, while the icy water nipped at her skin like sharp cold needles. Her breathing was shallow, her throat constricted by nervousness and raw from the salt water. Her hands were numb and bluey-white, but she commanded them to pull faster through the sea.

A thin ray of sun struggled through the cloud, and slowly burned a small hole. It was not long before they could see the black volcanic peaks of Big Diomede Island looming ahead. Soon they were close enough to see the shore. It had been over an hour and a half since she started.

Then, as they'd been warned, they hit a strong current. Not only did it push them north of the island, it was much, much colder than the water they'd been in. Later, Lynne found out that the water temperature dropped from 42 to 38°F (5.5 to 3.3°C). At those temperatures, every degree dramatically increased the danger of hypothermia. Her teeth began to chatter and chills shivered up her spine. It was unbearably cold, so cold it hurt.

But the shore looked so close. She'd been swimming for almost two hours by then and was bone weary. When she turned to get a breath, she saw the Soviet crew pointing to a snowbank south of where she was headed. Vladimir McMillan told her the welcoming party was waiting for her there. In order to meet them, she would have to swim precious extra minutes against this bone-chilling current.

It was very tempting to give up.

Lynne knew that if she didn't push on, she'd regret it for the rest of her life. But she also knew that there was a point where it's too dangerous to continue—no swim is worth risking your life over. The snowbank where the Soviets stood was at least 10 minutes of hard, fast swimming away. Did she have it in her? Could she make it?

Even her hands were as gray as a dead person's now, her shoulders a dark angry blue, her arms a bloodless white.

Concerned for her safety, Dr. Keatinge coaxed her to the right, toward the nearest shore. Instead, she swung left, swimming parallel to the land. "It's all the way, or no way," she shouted. The crew cheered and clapped, encouraging her, though the doctors were worried. The current pushed her back one stroke for every two she took. Fatigue numbed her and the cold bit into her last reservoir of energy. Still, inch by inch, she moved closer to the bank.

She glimpsed people slipping down the icy bank to meet her at the water's edge. The *umiaks* zoomed ahead and landed on small wooden ramps the Soviets had laid out for them.

Suddenly the ocean floor rose up beneath her. She was so tired she had to use her hands to climb out, but slipped backward even so. Three men leaned over as far as they could, encouraging her in Russian. Warm hands grabbed her shoulders and pulled her forward.

Once on land, her legs were so weak they wobbled. A man threw his jacket over her and someone wrapped a heavy blanket around her. McMillan kissed both of her cheeks in the customary Russian way.

"She needs to get warm," Dr. Keatinge said, supporting her arm. Now that Lynne was out of the water, chilly air blasted her wet skin. Her bare feet slipped on the icy ground. She was no longer generating any heat.

But the enthusiastic crowd pulled her along. This was a historic day. McMillan told her that his mother was Russian and his father American. As a result of Lynne's swim, he felt the two halves of himself come together for the first time in his life. He introduced her to the media and dignitaries: the Soviet Press, television crews, the national swim coach, the governor of Siberia, a KGB officer, a military commander, and three Siberian Inuit doctors.

The Soviets welcomed her warmly, but Lynne was growing colder and colder. Her Soviet hosts pulled her one way, while her doctor pulled her toward the medical tent.

Then McMillan told her the Soviet media wanted to hold a press conference.

Standing on the frozen beach, Lynne felt her temperature dropping, but struggled to answer their questions. Her focus kept slipping, and she had to ask them to repeat themselves. Her words slurred out of her numb lips.

The conversation got more and more complicated as they asked questions that had been saved during 48 years of silence between the two countries. They wanted her to speak for the entire US population, to tell them what the public thought, not the politicians. *Did the Americans really hate the Soviets?* they asked.

Even though her teeth were chattering, Lynne knew it was important to answer. But how could she possibly answer such a big question? With Vladimir McMillan translating, she explained what had motivated her swim. She then added, "I would not have swum here if I believed this was the evil empire.... We need to become friends. That is why I did this; that is why we did this." She pointed to her team. The Soviet press nodded their heads in agreement, contemplating what she'd said.

Meanwhile, the doctors could see she was staggering around clumsily. They finally pulled her away to the medical tent. Inside, a woman was waiting for her, holding out a blanket. McMillan explained that she was a doctor.

Dr. Keatinge and Dr. Nyboer crowded into the tent behind her. The Soviet doctor, seeing her blue lips, gestured to Lynne that she should take off her wet bathing suit. Lynne was suddenly embarrassed and pretended she didn't understand. After a few moments, the other woman realized the problem and waved the men out of the tent.

The preheated sleeping bag was wonderfully warm, but once she climbed in, violent shivering gripped her body. Her whole body shook, her breath shallow and rapid as her body struggled for air. The Soviet doctor gave her hot packs, which Lynne put close to the areas that cool down fastest: under her arms, behind her neck, and between her legs.

Outside, the two crews gathered around lavish buffet tables that had been set up on the beach. While Lynne shivered, the Soviet and American crews enjoyed a Siberian picnic. Waiters in uniforms served hot tea in china cups. Everyone laughed and tried to communicate through a mixture of Russian, English, and gestures.

Inside the tent, Lynne slowly heated up. It took a full hour before her temperature was normal. With her mind clear again, she introduced herself to the Soviet doctor. "What's your name?" she asked.

"Rita Zakharova," the woman replied and took out family

photos. Lynne pointed, asking if these were her children, but the woman shook her head. "*Nyet*," she replied. She pointed to herself and said, "I *babushka*."

Lynne frowned. Was her brain still confused by the cold? Was this woman saying she was a headscarf? "You're a...*babushka*?" she repeated.

"Yes," the woman answered. "Grandchildren."

Then Lynne got it—*babushka* means grandmother in Russian, as well as scarf. The Soviet government really had provided everything she asked for, including her very own *babushka*.

Dr. Zakharova offered her a gift of a hand-painted lacquer bowl. Overcome, Lynne searched for something to give in return, but all she had were her goggles and bathing cap. She offered these to the doctor, who accepted them as if they were treasures. The two women hugged and Lynne got dressed. Then Dr. Zakharova told her she could go outside and join the party.

FOUR MONTHS AFTER LYNNE'S BERING STRAIT CROSSING, the Soviet president, Mikhail Gorbachev, and the American president, Ronald Reagan, signed the first treaty to reduce their numbers of nuclear weapons. The historic meeting was televised.

From her home in California, Lynne watched as President Gorbachev said, "It took one brave American by the name of Lynne Cox just two hours to swim from one of our countries to the other. We saw on television how sincere and friendly the meeting was between our people and the Americans when she stepped onto the Soviet shore. She proved by her courage how close to each other our peoples live."

Lynne Cox went on to perform many more death-defying swims, often to promote goodwill among nations. She met both

Pope John Paul II and President Reagan, and was inducted into the International Swimming Hall of Fame.

In 2001, at 44 years old, she set another world record as the first person to swim a mile in Antarctic waters. Two years later, *Glamour* magazine named Lynne their Woman of the Year. After working as a research librarian for several years, Lynne now coaches, gives speeches and workshops, and writes. For the future, she's planning three new swims. She won't give any details, except to say they will be "risky."

Selected Sources

A Long Walk Home

Broome, Richard. *Aboriginal Australians: Black Responses to White Dominance 1788–1994.* 2nd ed. St. Leonards, NSW: Allen and Unwin, 1994.

Haebich, Anna. *Broken Circles: Fragmenting Indigenous Families 1800–2000.* North Freemantle, Western Australia: Freemantle Arts Centre Press, 2000.

Pilkington, Doris (Nugi Garimara). *Follow the Rabbit-Proof Fence.* Brisbane: University of Queensland Press, 1996.

Reconciliation and Social Justice Library. *Bringing Them Home: Report of the National Inquiry into the Separation of Aboriginal and Torres Strait Island Children from Their Families.* Chapter 7: Western Australia. Accessed at www.austlii.edu.au/au/special/rsjproject/ rsjlibrary/hreoc/stolen/stolen13.html.

Rafting across the Pacific

Heyerdahl, Thor. *The Kon-Tiki Expedition: By Raft across the South Seas.* Translated by F.H. Lyon. London: George Allen & Unwin Ltd., 1950.

Heyerdahl, Thor and Christopher Ralling. *Kon-Tiki Man: An Illustrated Biography of Thor Heyerdahl.* Vancouver: Douglas & McIntyre, 1991.

Special Delivery

Brown, Henry. *Narrative of the Life of Henry Box Brown, Written by Himself.* Electronic edition. Manchester: Lee and Glynn, 1851. Accessed at http://docsouth.unc.edu/neh/brownbox/brownbox.html

Brown, Henry and Charles Stearns. *Narrative of Henry Box Brown, Who Escaped from Slavery Enclosed in a Box 3 Feet Long and 2 Wide. Written from a Statement of Facts Made by Himself. With Remarks upon the Remedy for Slavery.* Electronic edition. Boston: Abner Forbes, 1849. Accessed at http://docsouth.unc.edu/neh/boxbrown/boxbrown.html

Wolff, Cynthia Griffin. "Passing Beyond the Middle Passage: Henry 'Box' Brown's Translations of Slavery." *Massachusetts Review* (Spring 1996), vol. 37, no. 1.

Alone above the Atlantic

Lovell, Mary S. *Straight On till Morning: The Biography of Beryl Markham.* New York: St. Martin's Press, 1987.

Markham, Beryl. *The Illustrated West with the Night.* New York: Stewart, Tabori & Chang, 1942; reprint 1983.

Trzebinksi, Errol. *The Lives of Beryl Markham: Out of Africa's Hidden Free Spirit and Denys Finch Hatton's Last Great Love.* New York: Norton, 1993.

The Greatest Traveler in the Medieval Muslim World

Dunn, Ross E. *The Adventures of Ibn Battuta: A Muslim Traveler of the 14th Century.* Rev. ed. Berkeley: University of California Press, 2005.

Mackintosh-Smith, Tim, ed. *The Travels of Ibn Battutah.* London: Picador, 2002.

Lost in a Green Hell

Smith, Anthony. *The Lost Lady of the Amazon: The Story of Isabela Godin and Her Epic Journey.* New York: Carroll & Graf, 2003.

Wakefield, Celia. *Searching for Isabel Godin: An Ordeal on the Amazon: Tragedy and Survival.* Berkeley: Creative Arts, 1999.

Whitaker, Robert. *The Mapmaker's Wife.* Cambridge: Basic Books, 2004. www.themapmakerswife.com

The Dead Man's March

Helly, Dorothy O. *Livingstone's Legacy: Horace Waller and Victorian Mythmaking.* Athens, OH: Ohio University Press, 1987.

Pakenham, Thomas. *The Scramble for Africa: The White Man's Conquest of the Dark Continent from 1876 to 1912.* New York: Random House, 1991.

Simpson, Donald. *Dark Companions: The African Contribution to the European Exploration of East Africa.* London: Paul Elek, 1975.

Stanley, Sir Henry M. *How I Found Livingstone: Travels, Adventures, and Discoveries in Central Africa.* London: Sampson Low, Marston, Searle & Rivington [1874–1890?].

Thomas, H.B. "The Death of Dr. Livingstone: Carus Farrar's Narrative." *The Uganda Journal* (September 1950), vol. 14, no. 2.

Into the Frozen Unknown

Bumsted, J.M. *The Peoples of Canada: A Pre-Confederation History.* 2nd ed. Don Mills, ON: Oxford, 2003.

Harrison, Keith. "Samuel Hearne, Matonabbee, and the 'Esquimaux Girl': Cultural Subjects, Cultural Objects." *Canadian Review of Comparative Literature* (1995), vol. 22, nos. 3–4.

Hearne, Samuel. *A Journey from Prince of Wales's Fort in Hudson's Bay to the Northern Ocean, 1769, 1770, 1771, 1772.* Accessed from www.canadiana.org/ECO/ItemRecord/35434?id=5ceebff6b92d7343

McGoogan, Kenneth. *Ancient Mariner: The Amazing Adventures of Samuel Hearne, the Sailor Who Walked to the Arctic Ocean.* Toronto: HarperCollins, 2003.

Crossing a War Zone

Hegi, Ursula. *Tearing the Silence: On Being German in America.* New York: Simon & Schuster, 1997.

Hoffman, Seigfried. Personal letters. Seigfried Hoffman to Barbara Hoffmann, February 17, 1986; Seigfried Hoffmann to Tanja Hoffmann, August 28, 1986; Seigfried Hoffmann to Tanja and Barbara Hoffmann, October 26, 1986; Seigfried Hoffmann to Barbara Hoffmann, April 30, 1987. Private collection, Hoffmann family, Vancouver, BC.

Kater, Michael H. *Hitler Youth.* Cambridge, MA.: Harvard University Press, 2004.

Tipton, Frank B. *A History of Modern Germany since 1815.* Berkeley: University of California Press, 2003.

Cold War Swim

Cox, Lynne. *Swimming to Antarctica.* Orlando, FL: Harcourt, 2004.

International Swimming Hall of Fame. www.ishof.org

"Cox, Lynne." *Current Biography Yearbook 2004* (September 2004), vol. 65, no. 9.

Kort, Michelle. "The Big Chill." *Women's Sports & Fitness* (April 1993), vol. 15, no. 3.

Dutter, Greg. "Taking the Plunge." *Biography Magazine* (December 2003).

Index

true stories from the edge

Acknowledgments

I would like to thank Tanja Hoffmann, Barb Hargreaves, and Linda Hoffmann for graciously giving me access to family papers and sharing memories. I only hope the effort has been worth your while. Special thanks to Valerie Burnett for research assistance, to the Bodleian Library for access to their records and to Marjory Muil for getting me through the Bodleian doors. To my first reader, Clinton Swanson, you've gone above and beyond. My editors, Pam Robertson and Elizabeth McLean, have worked wonders; all errors are my own. Finally, heartfelt thanks to all the folk at Annick Press for taking the risk.

About the Author

ANTONIA BANYARD made her first "crossing" at four years old when her family emigrated from Zambia, Africa to Canada. Since then, she has rafted the Zambezi River, hiked across (very) small mountains, canoed cold lakes, and flown across oceans and continents to Singapore, Brazil, England, and Australia. Most of the time, she travels by reading books.

She began writing in grade two and by grade five was working on five novels at once. She didn't finish any, and only one was longer than a few pages. However, since then she has written poetry, short stories, a novel, and essays. Her work has been published in Canada, the United States, England, and Australia. She lives in Vancouver, BC.